CONTENTS

THIS BOOK BELONGS TO . . . .

CHILDREN'S PICTORIAL BOOK
OF
KNOWLEDGE

Compiled and written by Jenny J Hunter

Illustrated by Steve Stock

© PETER HADDOCK LIMITED
BRIDLINGTON ENGLAND
ISBN 0–7105–0649–X

SPACE AND THE UNIVERSE

What is the Universe?

Bang! Crash! Boom!

Most astronomers believe that the Universe began with a violent explosion about 15,000 million years ago.

This huge explosion, which scientists called the 'Big Bang', scattered hot gases in all directions and eventually galaxies, stars and planets formed.

The Universe is made up of all the galaxies and the space around them.

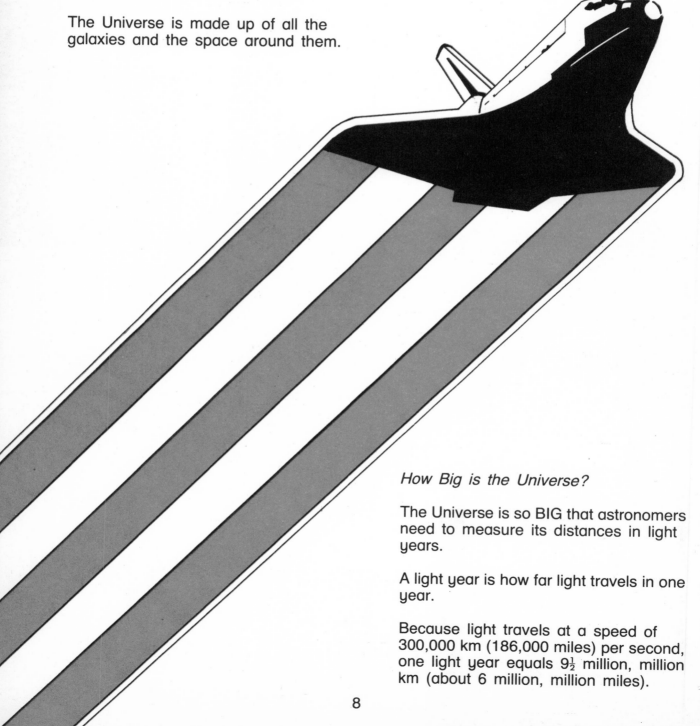

How Big is the Universe?

The Universe is so BIG that astronomers need to measure its distances in light years.

A light year is how far light travels in one year.

Because light travels at a speed of 300,000 km (186,000 miles) per second, one light year equals $9\frac{1}{2}$ million, million km (about 6 million, million miles).

and . . .

the Universe is getting BIGGER

Scientists are able to measure the speed
of stars in our part of the Universe to
compare with the speed of stars in more
distant parts and have concluded that the
Universe is expanding as the stars and
galaxies fly away from each other.

Galaxies

There are millions of galaxies in the night
sky. Each galaxy has millions of stars
clustered together and held by gravity.
The largest galaxies can have a million,
million stars grouped together.

9

Getting Together

Galaxies are found in groups and are recognised by the shape they make. The four main types are Spiral Galaxies, Elliptical (egg-shaped) Galaxies, Barred Spirals and Irregular Galaxies. The force of gravity helps them to keep their shapes.

Some of the galaxies have been given names. Our own galaxy, The Milky Way, is a Spiral Galaxy and is quite a small one with only some 20 galaxies clustered together.

The Virgo cluster is huge, with about 1000 galaxies in it.

How Close is Close?

The Andromeda Spiral is one of the nearest galaxies to the Milky Way. It is estimated to be about 2.2 million light years away and yet can be seen by the naked eye. Amazing!

Star Constellations

The word 'constellation' comes from the Latin word 'stella' which means star.

A constellation is a group of stars that seem to be joined up to make the outline shape of an animal, object or person.

All the stars visible from Earth lie within a constellation. Astronomers have identified 88 constellations. The one called The Plough is easy to spot; others are more difficult to find.

THE PLOUGH

So What is a Star?

A star is a cloud of hydrogen gas kept together by its own gravity. A nuclear reaction takes place and the star becomes very hot and shines more brightly as it gets hotter.

The stars we see in the night sky are distant suns.

Which Star is Nearest To Us?

An important star. Our own Sun.

The Sun is the closest star to the Earth.

Scientists are able to study it to help them to learn more about other stars much further away.

The Sun is 150 million km (93 million miles) away and the Sun's light takes 8 minutes to reach us.

The second nearest star is called Proxima Centauri and its light takes $4\frac{1}{4}$ light years to reach Earth.

Star Sizes

Many stars in the Universe are bigger than our Sun. They are known as blue giants. The biggest star is thought to be 1,000 million km (621 million miles) in diameter, over 700 times bigger than our Sun.

Stars smaller than the Sun are called red dwarfs and the smallest stars are white dwarfs.

12

The Heaviest Star

When a big star has no more fuel (gas) to burn it starts to collapse and, as it shrinks, its atoms squash ever more tightly together into an incredibly heavy ball of atoms called a neutron star.

The Death of a Star

When the hydrogen gas in the middle of a star is burning up the star begins to die. The ball of gas spreads out to become a red giant star which then cools and shrinks to become a white dwarf. Eventually the star 'dies' and becomes an almost invisible black dwarf.

Sometimes the largest stars explode, throwing off the outer layers of the star in clouds of glowing gas and are known as supernovas. New stars will form from these gas clouds.

Into a 'Black Hole'

The force of gravity pulling into the neutron star is so great that not even light rays can escape. Because the light cannot leave the star we are not able to see it; the star has become a 'black hole'.

The 'Star' That is Not a Star

'Shooting stars' are really tiny pieces of rock called meteors. When a meteor reaches Earth's atmosphere it begins to glow white hot and then burns up, giving off the streaks of light which we call 'shooting stars'.

A Strange Truth

Every day, minute particles of dust from burnt-out meteors settle on the Earth's surface making Earth heavier.

ASTEROIDS CERES AND VESTA

STONY–IRON METEORITE

A Collision in Space

There are thousands of small planets, called asteroids, revolving round the Sun and when these planets (asteroids) collide, huge lumps of rock fall to Earth. These rocks are called meteorites and make large craters in the ground. The largest meteorite fell on the continent of Africa thousands and thousands of years ago. It weighed about 60 tonnes. Luckily, massive meteorites rarely hit Earth – only once in every 10,000 years!

But every year many small meteorites do hit Earth, most of them falling harmlessly into the sea.

Snowballs in the Sky

When we see a comet it looks like a bright dot with a long shiny tail. Scientists believe that comets are balls of frozen water and gas, mixed with dust particles and rock.

There are said to be 100,000 million comets circling around the Sun.

A comet has two parts, a head and a tail. The head is the 'dirty snowball' and the tail is thought to be made of gas and dust forced out of the head by the Sun's radiation. Comets do not give out light but reflect the light of the Sun. As the comet gets nearer to Earth it glows more brightly and then fades as it hurtles far into space.

HALLEY'S COMET

Chinese Painting 168 BC

Comet depicted in
Poland 1600s

Halley's Comet 1066
Recorded on the Bayeux Tapestry

Halley's Comet

In 1682 Edmund Halley, Britain's Astronomer Royal, was watching the progress of a comet and after carefully checking his records decided that this particular comet was appearing once every 76 years. The same comet had been seen in England in 1066 just before the Battle of Hastings.

In 1986 a spacecraft was launched to provide data about Halley's Comet. Two thousand pictures were sent back, showing the Comet's shape and size. Halley's Comet was found to be twice as big as scientists had thought. It is nearly 10 miles long and 6 miles wide.

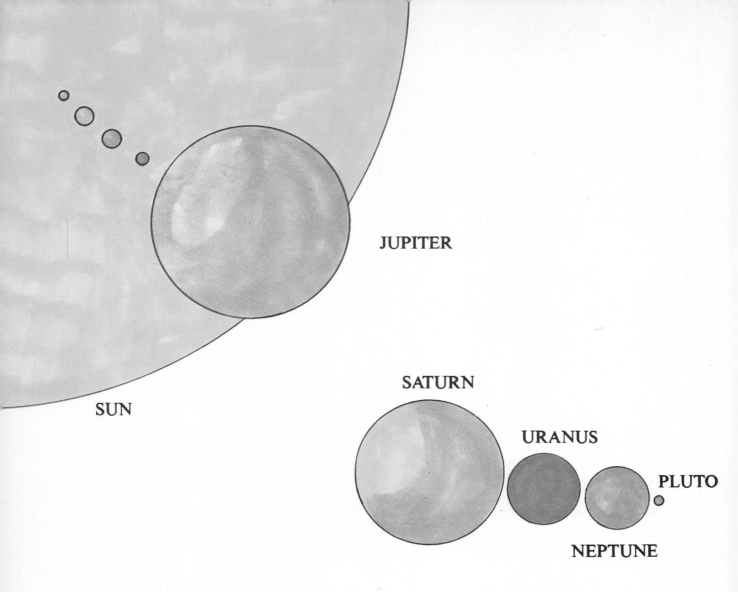

JUPITER

SUN

SATURN

URANUS

PLUTO

NEPTUNE

THE SOLAR SYSTEM

The Solar System

The Solar System is the name we give to the Sun's family of nine planets and their moons, all circling round (orbiting) the Sun, together with the comets and asteroids also in orbit round the Sun.

There are about 40,000 asteroids forming a ring around the Sun with Mercury, Venus, Earth and Mars nearest the Sun as the Inner Planets and Jupiter, Saturn, Uranus, Neptune and Pluto as the Outer Planets, farthest from the Sun.

Round and Round They Go!

Everything in the Solar System is on the move. The moons orbit (circle) their own planets; each planet spins on its axis as it circles the Sun; and the Sun also spins round. So the whole of the Solar System is moving around the galaxy in which it lies.

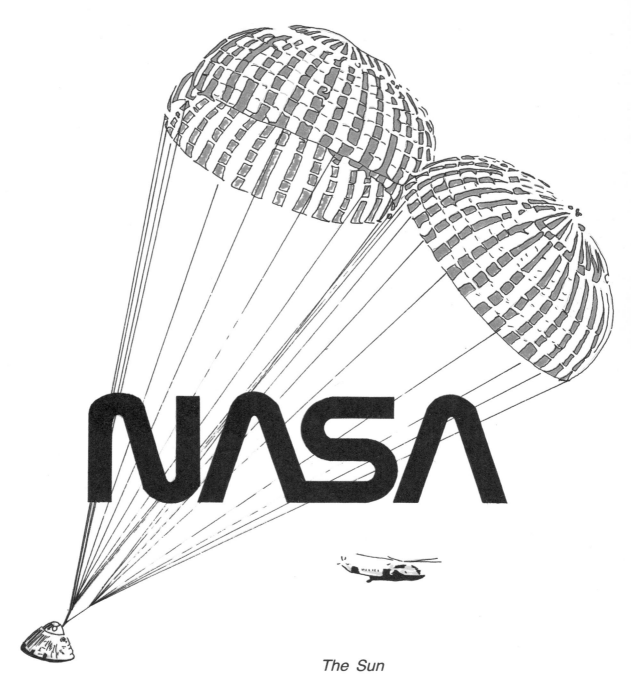

The Sun

The Sun is very much bigger than the planets in the Solar System. Try to imagine its size. If the Earth were the size of a pea, the Sun would be as large as a football.

The Sun is an ordinary star just like millions of others in the Milky Way but it is very important in our Solar System. The Sun is like a fiery ball in the sky, made up of hydrogen gas and giving off heat, light and energy as it burns.

Without the Sun there would be no life on Earth.

And All This From A Cloud

Many scientists believe that the Solar System was formed about 4,600 million years ago. The force of gravity pulled a huge cloud of gases and dust together in space. The Sun formed in the middle and planets grew from balls of gas around it.

The Incredibly Hot Sun

The gases on the surface of the Sun reach a temperature of 6000°C (10,800°F), but at the centre it is 15 million °C (27 million °F). Vast amounts of heat and light are given off by the gases on the Sun's surface but most of the heat and light is lost in space during the 8 minutes it takes for the Sun's light to reach Earth.

The Sun's harmful ultra-violet rays are filtered out by the ozone layer 24 km (15 miles) above the surface of the Earth.

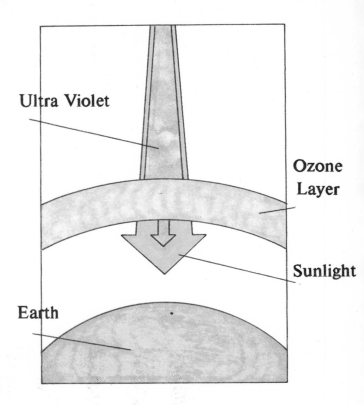

Ultra Violet

Ozone Layer

Sunlight

Earth

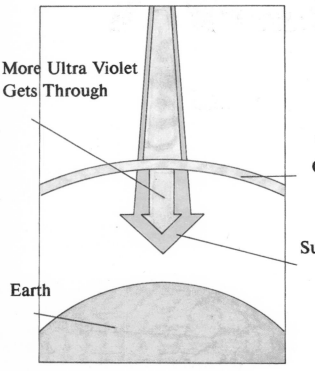

More Ultra Violet Gets Through

Thinner Ozone Layer

Sunlight

Earth

The Sun's Spectacular Show

Sometimes beautiful shining coloured lights, called aurorae, can be seen in the skies above the North and South Poles. They occur when dust particles hurtle from the Sun and collide with gases in the Earth's atmosphere.

The Northern Lights are called Aurora Borealis and the Southern lights are called Aurora Australis.

Sun Spots

At times, the surface of the Sun appears to have dark patches on it. These are called sunspots. Astronomers think that they are caused by areas of cooler gas on the Sun's surface which seem dark when compared with the rest of the brilliant surface.

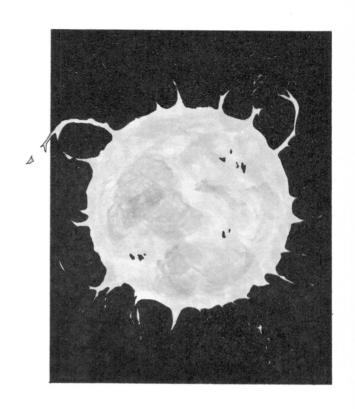

ANNULAR ECLIPSE OF THE SUN

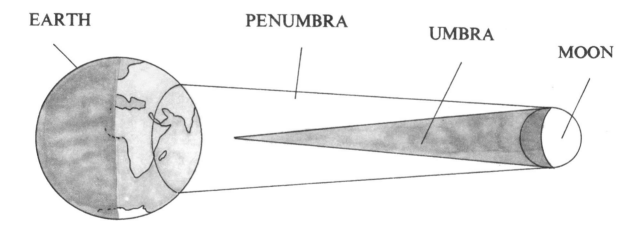

EARTH   PENUMBRA   UMBRA   MOON

An Eclipse of the Sun

Eclipses happen when the Sun, Moon and Earth are all in line with each other and the Moon blocks out the light from the Sun.

An eclipse may last for anything up to $7\frac{1}{2}$ minutes and, seen from Earth, looks like a shining white circle of light around a black space where the Sun had been.

19

Four Rocky Inner Planets

1 *Mercury*

Mercury is the nearest planet to the Sun and also the hottest with a daytime temperature more than 7 times hotter than any place on Earth. At night, the temperature drops to below freezing point because Mercury has no atmosphere to hold the heat. Mercury is the smallest of the inner planets and is solid like the Earth. Mercury travels round the Sun much faster than all the other planets and is named after the messenger of the Roman gods.

THE ROMAN GOD

MERCURY

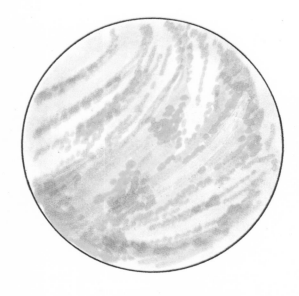

VENUS

2 *Venus – Odd One Out*

Venus is about the same size as the Earth with mountains and deserts on its surface. The atmosphere is made up of poisonous carbon dioxide gas and is so thick that it traps the heat and makes the planet very hot.

Venus is the brightest of the planets seen from Earth and rotates in the opposite direction from the rest of the planets. This means that the Sun rises in the West and sets in the East!

3 Planet Earth

Earth is unique because it is the only planet in the Solar System able to support life and, as far as it is known, is the only place in the whole of the universe to support life.

and in the Right Place

If the Earth were nearer the Sun it would be too hot for living things to survive and if it were further away from the Sun it would be too cold.

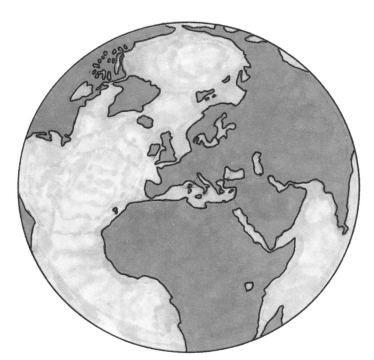

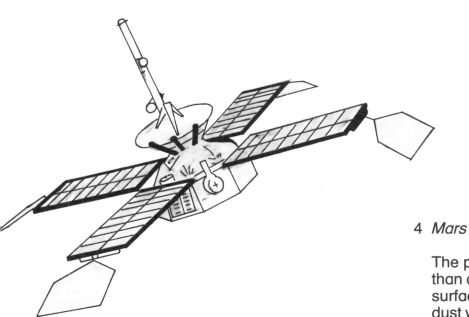

MARINER 4

4 Mars

The planet Mars is more like the Earth than any other of the Sun's planets. Its surface has a covering of brownish dust with craters and geological cracks which look like narrow, dry canals. It has mountains higher than Everest.

Un-manned spacecraft have landed on Mars but scientists believe that manned exploration of Mars is possible.

The Outer Planets

1 Jupiter – The Giant

Jupiter is the biggest planet in the Solar System – so large that all the other planets could fit inside it. Jupiter has a small rocky centre surrounded by a swirling mass of liquid hydrogen gas.

The red patch on Jupiter is called the Great Red Spot and is thought to be caused by a large cloud of gas rising from the planet's surface. Jupiter rotates amazingly quickly on its axis causing the equator to bulge out and making the planet look like a flattened ball.

JUPITER

SATURN

2 Saturn – The Ringed Planet

Saturn is the second largest planet in the Solar System and easily recognised by the beautiful glowing rings which surround it. The rings are made up of millions and millions of small particles of ice and rock.

Saturn itself is made up of helium and hydrogen gas and has the lowest density of any of the Solar System's planets.

Amazingly, Saturn would float if it were possible to find a large enough body of water in which to place it.

3 Uranus – The Tilted Planet

Uranus was first seen in 1781 by an amateur astronomer called William Herschel. Uranus is over 2,735 million km (1,700 million miles) away from the Sun and is therefore a very cold planet. It is mostly made up of hydrogen and helium and the methane gas present in its atmosphere makes it appear green when seen from Earth.

As recently as 1977, astronomers discovered that Uranus has dark rings around its equator.

Uranus is tilted on its side as it orbits the sun.

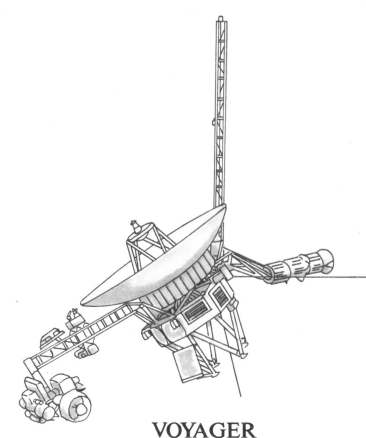

VOYAGER

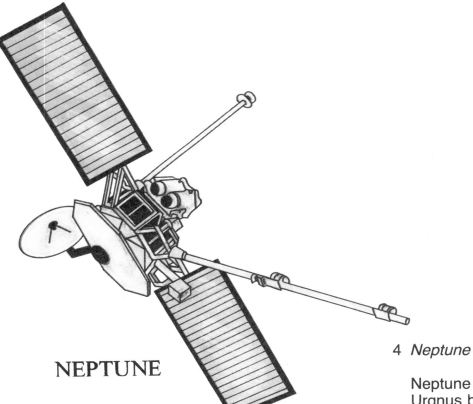

NEPTUNE

4 Neptune

Neptune is very much like the planet Uranus but is a little smaller. Neptune is more than 4,345 million km (2,700 million miles) from the Sun and is a very cold place indeed.

It takes Neptune 164 Earth years to travel once round the Sun.

5 *Pluto – The Furthest Planet?*

Pluto was first seen in 1930 and is the smallest and lightest planet in the Solar System being only 2,400 km (1,491 miles) in diameter. It is smaller than our moon.

Pluto is thought to be a solid planet, more like our Earth but it is so far away, 5,899 million km (3,666 million miles), that little is known about it.

Pluto's pathway round the Sun takes the shape of a flattened circle. Because of this different orbit, Pluto is now closer to the Sun than Neptune and it will be 1999 before Pluto once more becomes the furthest planet in the Solar System.

The Moon

The Moon is a natural satellite orbiting the Earth about 384,000 km (239,000 miles) away. It is much smaller and lighter than the Earth and takes 29 days to move round the Earth.

The Moon has no light of its own but reflects the light of the Sun. As the Moon travels around the Earth it appears to change shape and we call these different shapes the Phases of the Moon. The reason for this is that as the Earth orbits the Sun it shades the Moon so that different amounts of light are reflected.

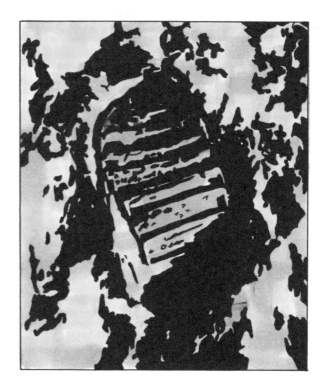

Man's First Footprint On The Moon

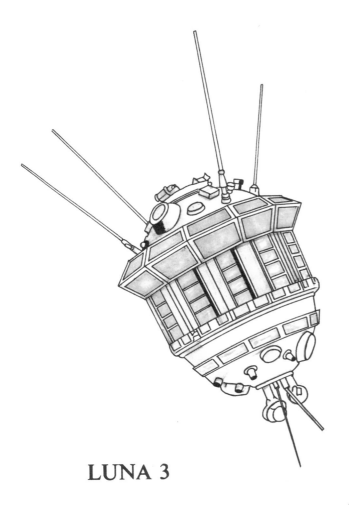

The same side of the Moon is always facing the Earth and, until 1959, when the Russian spacecraft, Luna 3, took photographs of the far side of the Moon, no-one knew what that side looked like.

The Moon has no atmosphere and no water, so no life is possible.

LUNA 3

More About the Moon

The Moon is made of rock with thousands and thousands of craters on its surface. There are large areas of flat, dusty plains and tall mountains. It is possible that the craters were formed by bubbles bursting on the lunar crust after volcanic activity millions of years ago.

It is the pull of Earth's gravity that keeps the Moon in orbit around it.

The Moon's gravity is only about one sixth of that on Earth and causes the tides in the oceans on Earth as the water is pulled towards the Moon.

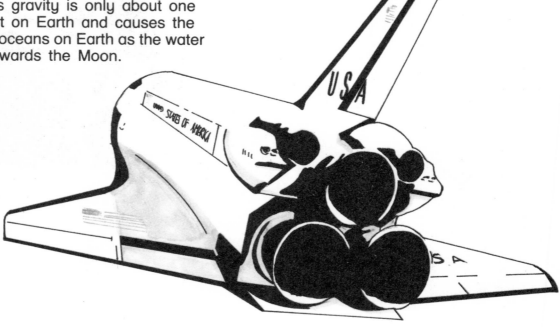

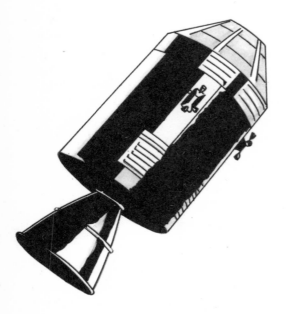

The American spacecraft Apollo 11 landed on the Moon in July 1969 and the astronaut Neil Armstrong was the first man on the Moon.

Various other successful Apollo missions have taken place and samples of lunar rock and dust have been brought back to Earth.

The Moon rocks were found to be more than 4,700 million years old, older than any of the Earth's rocks.

Undisturbed by Wind or Water

The rocks picked up by the astronauts had probably been lying in exactly the same place for over 3,000 million years.

1 Early astronomers believed that the Earth was the centre of the Universe.

2 The Polish astronomer, Nicolaus Copernicus, discovered that the Earth and the other planets orbit the Sun.

3 In 1608 Galileo Galilei was the first astronomer to use a telescope in his study of space.

4 It is possible to see the planets Mercury, Venus, Mars, Jupiter and Saturn with the naked eye.

5 Far out in space, away from the pull of gravity of planets, objects have no weight at all.

6 The first man-made satellite in space was the Russian Sputnik 1. In 1957 it was put into orbit round the Earth.

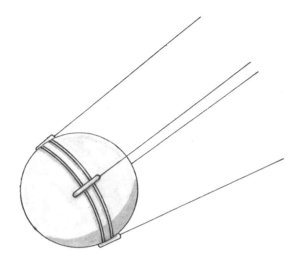

SPUTNIK 1957

7 Laika, a Russian dog, was the first traveller in space in 1957.

8 The first human space traveller was Yuri Gagarin in 1961. His journey lasted 89 minutes.

9 1971 saw the first space-station. It was the USSR's Salyut 1.

10 The American space shuttle first flew in 1981.

11 Un-manned spacecraft have been investigating the other planets in our Solar System since 1962.

12 The American spacecraft, Pioneer 10, launched in 1972, has now travelled beyond Pluto's orbit and out of our Solar System into the depths of space.

OUR PLANET — EARTH

Earth is the fifth largest planet of the Solar System and it is the third nearest to the Sun. The distance from the Sun is 150,000,000km (93,000,000 miles).

The Earth revolves in space once every 24 hours. It takes $364\frac{1}{4}$ days for the Earth to orbit once round the Sun.

Fast Facts

1. The Earth is not round, but flattens slightly at the North and South Poles and bulges at the Equator.
2. The Equator is an imaginary line around the middle of the Earth.
3. The distance round the Equator is 40,075km (24,903 miles).
4. The Earth weighs 6000 million, million, million tonnes.
5. Nearly $\frac{3}{4}$ of the Earth's surface is covered by water.
6. There is more land to the north of the Equator.
7. Most of the people on Earth live in the countries which lie north of the Equator.

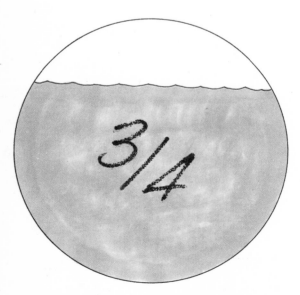

3/4 OF THE EARTH'S SURFACE IS COVERED IN WATER

The Beginning of the Earth

Scientists believe that our Earth was formed from a cloud of flaming dust and gases about 4,600 million years ago. The huge spinning mass of gases and dust became smaller and formed a hot molten ball.

Millions of years later, the surface cooled and hardened to form a thin crust of rock.

Inside the Earth

Studies by geologists (scientists who study the Earth) show that the Earth is made up of three different layers.

At the centre of the Earth is the core, surrounded by the next layer, called the mantle, and then the outer layer, the Earth's 'skin' or crust of rock.

The Core

The core is actually made up of two layers. The very centre of the Earth is called the inner core. This is a solid ball of nickel and iron about 2440km (1516 miles) across with a temperature almost as hot as that of the Sun. The inner core does not melt, but stays solid because of the weight and pressure of the Earth above.

The Mantle

Earth's mantle is a layer of hot liquid rock about 2800km (1739.92 miles) thick. Because the rock is at melting point the mantle has a mushy, putty-like texture.

The Crust

The surface of the Earth is made up of two types of crust – the continental and the oceanic.

Under the seas is the oceanic crust which is about 5km (3.1 miles) thick.

The continental crust is more than 30km (18.6 miles) thick beneath the mountains and it is the continental crust which forms the Earth's land masses.

The Floating Crust

Earth's crust is not one solid piece. It is broken into seven very large pieces and several smaller ones. These pieces are called plates. They float on the mantle of hot liquid beneath the crust.

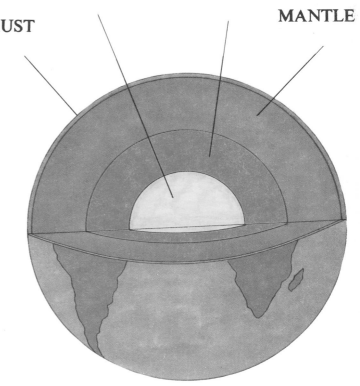

CRUST **SOLID CORE** **LIQUID CORE** **MANTLE**

The movement of the Earth's crust is called 'continental drift'.

More than 200 million years ago the continents were joined together.

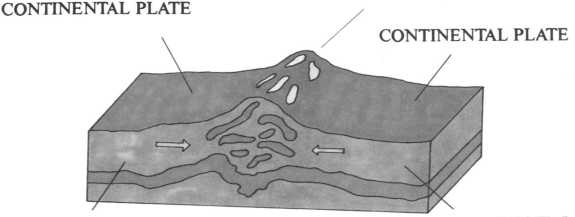

CONTINENTAL PLATE **FOLD MOUNTAINS** **CONTINENTAL PLATE**

CONTINENTAL CRUST **CONTINENTAL CRUST**

Collision Course – crashing plates

For millions of years the plates have drifted into and around each other. Where the plates crashed and collided the crust buckled and formed deep gashes or trenches in the ocean bed forcing the rocks up to make mountains. The Alps seem huge mountains to us, but they are really wrinkles in the Earth's 'skin'.

Sliding Plates

The plates can also slip past each other, under the sea as well as on land. When two plates try to slide past each other the rocky, jagged edges grind together. They may get stuck or 'locked-up' but, eventually, huge forces build up and pull them past each other in sudden jerks – these are earthquakes.

The cracks in the Earth's crust are called faults. In the USA the San Andreas Fault stretches from the Gulf of California for some 1100km (683.5 miles).

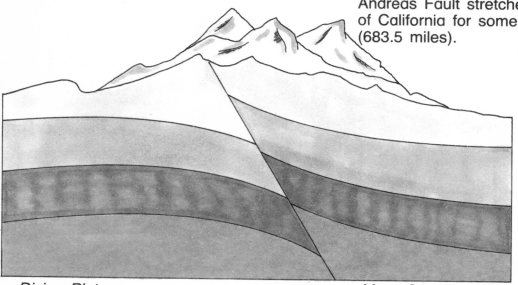

Diving Plates

Enormous heat and pressure build up when one plate dives under another and presses down into the Earth's mantle. The heat erupts to the surface as a series of volcanoes along the fault line.

More Crust

New crust is constantly being formed on the ocean floor. Soft, hot rock pushes up through the crack (fault) between two plates and as it cools, new rock is made.

The ridge in the middle of the Atlantic is gaining small amounts of rock each year.

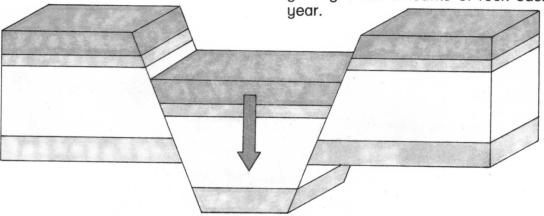

RIFT VALLEY CREATED BY A FAULT

The Changing Earth

Over millions of years, the surface of the Earth has been changing. Erosion by wind, water and ice has altered the landscape. Even today the Earth's shape is changing.

Man-Made Changes

Man also makes changes to the Earth's landscape in many different ways —

Forests are cut down.

Coal, slate and rock are quarried. Precious metal and minerals are mined.

Canals and waterways are constructed.

The courses of rivers are altered.

Lakes and reservoirs are created.

Land is reclaimed from the sea.

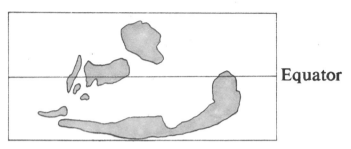

500 Million Years Ago

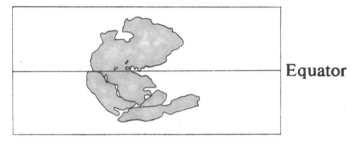

300 Million Years Ago

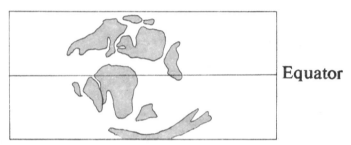

100 Million Years Ago

Earth's Atmosphere

The Earth is surrounded by an envelope of air, called the atmosphere.

The force of gravity holds the atmosphere around the Earth.

The atmosphere is made up of a mixture of different gases such as oxygen, nitrogen and carbon dioxide, as well as minute particles of dust and water vapour.

There are several layers to the atmosphere, the highest being about 8000km (4971.2 miles) above the surface of the Earth.

Into Thin Air

To reach the summit of the tallest mountains, climbers need extra oxygen because the air becomes thinner the higher you go.

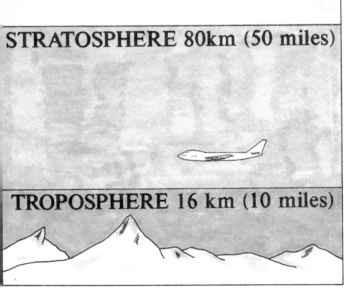

IONOSPHERE 500 km (310 miles)

STRATOSPHERE 80km (50 miles)

TROPOSPHERE 16 km (10 miles)

The Living Planet

It is the Sun's radiation and the mixture of gases and water vapour in the Earth's atmosphere that make life on Earth possible.

About 2000 million years ago, microscopic plants, called algae, began to appear. Plants breathe in carbon-dioxide and with the help of sunlight produce oxygen. All animals, including human beings, breathe in oxygen and breathe out carbon-dioxide.

Rocks, Mountains and Volcanoes

Rocks

The rocks of the Earth's crust belong to three main groups —

1 *Igneus Rock*

This type of rock was formed from hot, molten rock, called magma, deep inside the Earth's mantle.

The magma rose to the surface of the Earth where it cooled and hardened. Basalt and granite are igneus rocks.

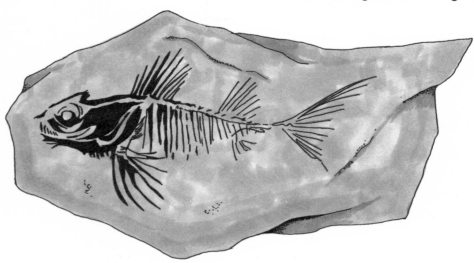

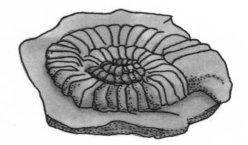

2 *Sedimentary Rocks*

Millions of years ago, sedimentary rock was formed under the oceans. Mud and sand particles, parts of plants, shells and the remains of sea creatures settled in layers on the sea bed. It took millions of years for the layers to compress together to form solid rock. Sandstone, chalk and limestone are examples of sedimentary rocks.

3 *Metamorphic Rocks*

This type of rock was formed when extreme heat and pressure caused changes to occur in both igneus and sedimentary rocks. Slate and marble are examples of metamorphic rock.

Rock Content

The rocks of the Earth's crust contain many different metals and minerals.

People have been mining gold, silver, tin, iron, copper and lead for thousands of years. The largest nugget (lump) of pure gold was found in 1869 in Australia.

Many of the minerals found in the rocks are used in everyday life. Salt (sodium chloride) has many uses.

Minerals contain a mixture of chemical substances, such as potassium, aluminium, calcium and magnesium.

Gemstones

Emeralds, rubies, sapphires and diamonds are some of the precious minerals to be found in the rocks of the Earth's crust.

The Cullinan diamond, found in South Africa in 1905, is the biggest diamond in the world.

EMERALDS

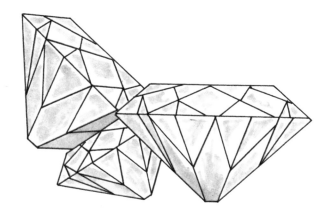

ROUND CUT DIAMONDS

Fossils

Fossils are the hardened remains of dead animals and plants, pressed into the rock layers of the Earth's crust. Fossils form when mud and sand gradually turn into stone. By studying fossils scientists have been able to discover what kind of life existed millions of years ago. The study of fossils is called paleontology.

Caves and Caverns

Caves and caverns occur naturally in the Earth's crust. Sea-caves are formed by the action of ocean waves and the stones and boulders which are hurled against the cliff.

Inland Caves

Inland caves are usually found in areas of limestone. Over the years water seeps into the earth, gradually wearing away the rock and limestone to form caves.

Icicles of Stone

In some caves beautiful 'icicles' called stalactites hang downwards. They are formed when the mineral deposits in water drips harden. Stalagmites form in the same way, growing upwards from the floor of the cave.

The Quaking, Shaking Earth

Earthquakes are caused by the movement of two plates of rock beneath the Earth's crust. Every year there are about one million earthquakes. Most of them are so small that they can be detected only by a seismograph (an instrument that measures the power of earthquakes). Most earthquakes occur in the 'Ring of Fire', which almost completely circles the Pacific Ocean, and in a second earthquake line called the Alpine Belt. This stretches eastwards from Spain, through the Mediterranean to Turkey, on to the Himalayas and as far as South-East Asia.

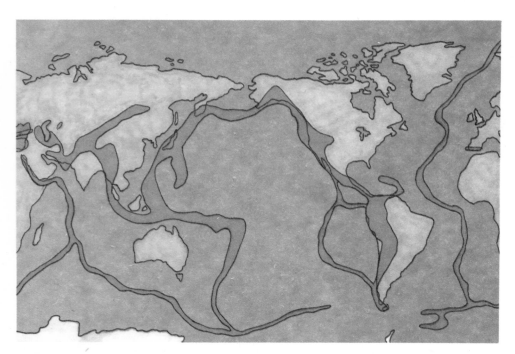

EARTHQUAKE AREAS OF THE WORLD

Great Sea Waves

Earthquakes occur under the sea as well as on land.

Most do little harm but others cause 'tidal waves' called tsunamis. A tsunami is a series of waves which race across the ocean. As the waves near land they slow down and the wave height increases before crashing down on to the shore.

The effects of a tsunami are usually disastrous. In 1946 the tsunami which struck Hawaii killed 173 people.

34

Mountains

Mountains cover about one fifth of the surface of the Earth.

Mount Everest is the world's highest mountain. It is 8,848m (29,028ft) above sea level.

Although mountain ranges are millions of years old, some are much older than others. The mountains in the Highlands of Scotland were formed about 400 million years ago, but the Alps are only about 15 million years old.

Mountains slowly change shape as they get older and are worn away by rain, wind and ice.

Underwater Mountains

Some of the world's biggest mountains are on the sea bed. Some undersea mountains are taller than those on land. Many islands are really the tops of mountains rising out of the water.

The Caribbean Islands are a chain of islands that are the tips of an underwater mountain range.

The Making of Mountains

Mountains are formed by movements in the Earth's rocky crust. The layers of rocks are pushed upward, folding and breaking to form different shapes or types of mountains. As time passes, erosion by frost and rain causes the mountains to split and valleys and cliffs are formed.

Some mountains are formed by volcanic eruptions. The molten rock which bubbles out through holes in the Earth's crust builds up, layer by layer, until it finally becomes a mountain. Mount Vesuvius, in Italy, is a volcanic mountain.

Volcanic mountains can build up under the ocean. The Hawaiian Islands are volcanic mountains.

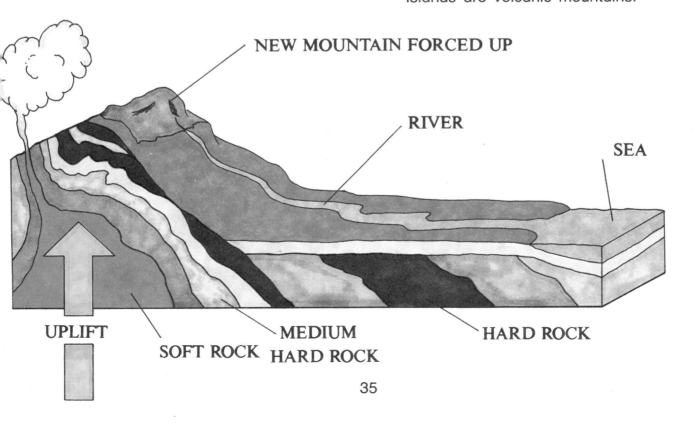

NEW MOUNTAIN FORCED UP

RIVER

SEA

UPLIFT

SOFT ROCK

MEDIUM HARD ROCK

HARD ROCK

Volcanoes

The earth has more than 600 active volcanoes. Many of them are under the sea.

When a volcano explodes (erupts) lava and clouds of gas, dust and ash are thrown out. Lava is hot molten rock.

Extinct Volcanoes

Some volcanoes have ceased to erupt. They have become extinct or dead.

Krakatoa – The Exploding Island

In 1883 a volcano on the Indonesian island of Krakatoa erupted. The noise from the explosion was so great that it was heard almost 5000km (nearly 3000 miles) away in Australia. The effects of the blast were spectacular as well as devastating. Ash and rock flew 80km (50 miles) up into the air. Winds carried the volcanic dust around the world, causing beautiful sunsets.

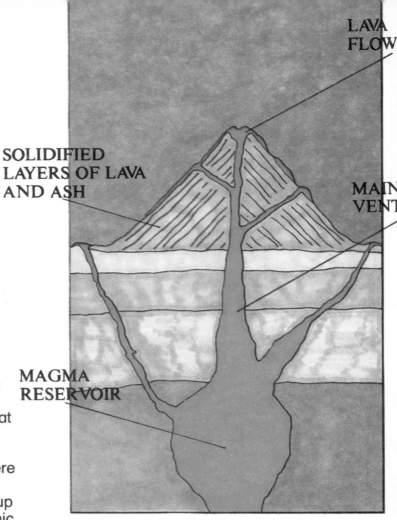

LAVA FLOW

SOLIDIFIED LAYERS OF LAVA AND ASH

MAIN VENT

MAGMA RESERVOIR

A giant tsunami ('tidal wave') raced across the ocean, crashed down on the islands of Java and Sumatra and killed 36,000 people. When everything was peaceful again, the island of Krakatoa had vanished – just a few jagged rocks remained.

Hot Water Springs and Geysers

Deep under the Earth's surface are underground rivers and springs. The water is heated to boiling point by hot volcanic rock inside the Earth. Pressure builds up and the hot water meets the cold water seeping down from the surface of the earth, forcing it upwards to explode as a jet of hot water and steam. A geyser has been created.

In some places the ground 'bubbles' and in others water collects in steaming pools. New Zealand's islands are part of a volcanic range of mountains and contain many geysers and hot springs.

HOT SPRINGS

EARTH'S WONDERFUL WATER

Where did it come from?

As the gases that formed the Earth cooled, a chemical reaction took place between hydrogen and oxygen. Liquid particles formed in a thick cloud around the Earth.

The Longest Shower of Rain

When the rocks of the Earth's surface cooled, the water poured from the clouds as the Earth's first shower of rain.

It lasted for 60,000 years.

There were terrible floods and the first seas were made. Low land between the mountains was flooded, lakes and rivers formed and the oceans filled with water.

Amazing – but true

Our water is 300,000 million years old. Earth keeps all the water ever created to be used and re-used.

RAIN CYCLE

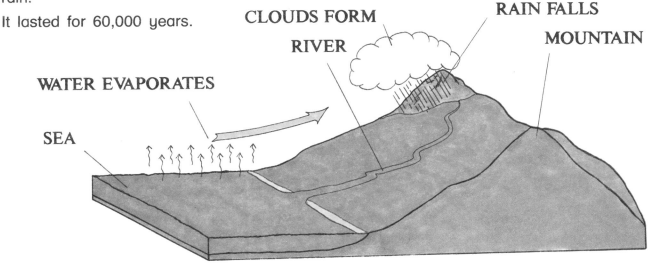

CLOUDS FORM

RIVER

RAIN FALLS

MOUNTAIN

WATER EVAPORATES

SEA

But how?

This happens because of the natural 'water-cycle'.

The heat of the Sun draws up water from the oceans and seas as water vapour. The winds blow it over the land where it cools and falls as rain. The rivers carry the water back to the seas and in this way the world's water is recycled over and over again.

Would you Believe?

a) The Earth's atmosphere contains enough water to cover the world with 25mm (1in) of rain, if it all fell at one time.

b) Over 97% of the water on Earth lies in the oceans.

SEAS AND OCEANS

Salt in the Sea

The seas are salty because rivers wash salt and other minerals into them. Some seas are saltier than others.

The Dead Sea

The Dead Sea, between Jordan and Israel, is so salty that no fish can live in it. It is very difficult for people to dive or swim under water but very easy to float on the surface.

The World's Oceans

About 71% of the Earth's surface is covered by oceans.

The oceans are divided by the continents and islands.

The Pacific is the largest ocean, covering almost one third of the Earth's surface.

The Atlantic is the second largest, only half as big as the Pacific.

The Indian Ocean is the third largest and the Arctic is the smallest.

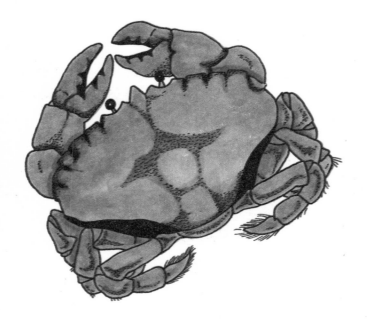

The World's Seas

The oceans are divided into areas and their seas are near coasts and islands.

The Pacific Ocean has the Coral and South China Seas.

The Atlantic has the Mediterranean and the Caribbean Seas.

The Indian Ocean has the Persian Gulf and the Red Sea.

The Arctic Ocean has Hudson Bay and Baffin Bay within it.

There are also many smaller seas throughout the world.

On The Move

The water in the seas keeps moving. The heat from the Sun is absorbed by the oceans and spread across the world by huge flows of water, called currents.

One of the most powerful currents is the warm Gulf Stream which flows across the Atlantic Ocean from the Caribbean at a speed of about 6km (4 miles) an hour.

The Daily Tides

The tides are caused by the gravitational pull of the Sun and the Moon. The highest Spring tides occur when the Moon and the Sun are pulling on the same side of the Earth.

SPRING TIDES

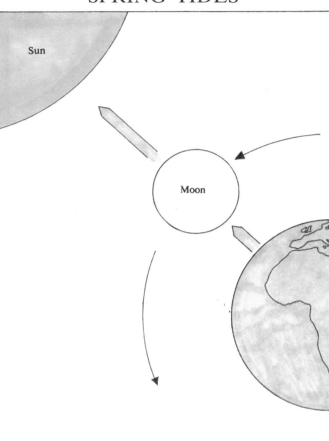

NEAP TIDES

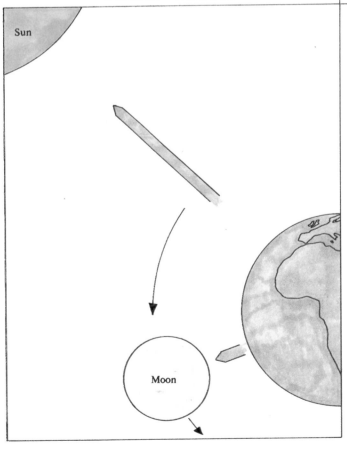

FROZEN WATER

Glaciers and Icebergs

Almost three-quarters of the world's fresh water is frozen inside glaciers.

Glaciers are slow-moving masses or 'rivers' of ice formed in mountain valleys.

In some places, the ice sheets are more than 3000m (9842ft) thick.

IF the glaciers melted it is thought that the water from them would raise the sea level by about 60m (nearly 200ft).

The Lambert Glacier, in the Antarctic, is the largest glacier in the world. It is over 400km (248.56 miles) in length.

Icebergs

When glaciers reach the sea, blocks of ice break off and float away – these are icebergs.

Drifting icebergs are a danger to ships. Only about one-tenth of an iceberg shows above water: the rest is hidden below the surface.

In 1912 the passenger liner 'Titanic' sank after hitting an iceberg and 1490 people were drowned. Since then the International Ice Patrol has watched the movement of icebergs and is able to warn ships of any danger.

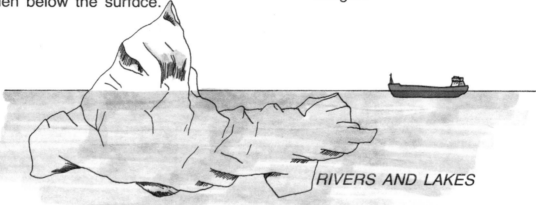

RIVERS AND LAKES

Rivers

Rivers contain fresh water.

Most rivers begin in mountainous areas and flow down to the sea. Muddy flatlands, called deltas, may form where rivers meet the sea. Some rivers are so long that they flow through more than one country.

River Facts

1. The Nile, in Africa, is the longest river in the world. It is 6670km (4144 miles) long.

2. The Amazon, in South America, is the second-longest river at 6437km (4000 miles).

3. The Mississippi/Missouri, in North America, is the third-longest at 5520km (3430 miles).

Waterfalls

1. The world's highest waterfall is in Venezuela. The Angel Falls are 979m (3212ft) high.

2. The Tugela Falls, in South Africa, are 948m (3110ft) high.

3. Niagara Falls, in North America, are thousands of years old.

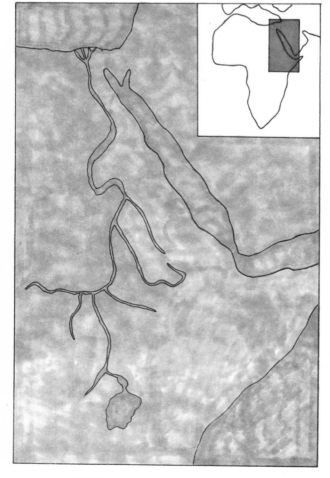

THE RIVER NILE

Lakes

Lakes usually contain fresh water. Some lakes, such as the Caspian, contain salt water and are really inland seas.

Lake Superior, in Canada, is the world's largest freshwater lake. It covers an area of nearly 82,500 sq km (31,845 square miles).

The world's deepest lake is in the USSR. In some places Lake Baikal is over 1900m (6233.5ft) deep.

FORESTS

Forests cover about one quarter of the Earth's land surface. There are three main types of forest. Most of them are rain forests.

Coniferous Forest (Cone-Bearing Trees)

Nearly all conifers are evergreen. Conifer trees have 'needle-like' leaves. Some conifers such as larches, do shed their leaves (needles).

PINE CONE AND NEEDLES

ACORN AND OAK LEAVES

Coniferous forests grow in the colder, northern regions of the world and high up on mountains. Coniferous forests are found across North America, northern Europe and Asia and on mountain ranges, such as the Alps and the Rockies. Coniferous forests provide most of the world's timber and paper.

Deciduous Forest (Broad-leaved)

Deciduous, broad-leaved forests are found in parts of the world that have warm, temperate (moderate) climates.

Oak, ash, elm, beech and birch are examples of deciduous broad-leaved trees.

They shed their leaves in autumn.

Rain Forest

Rain forests contain broad-leaved evergreen trees.

Rain forests grow in hot, wet regions. Hundreds of species of trees, shrubs and plants are found in the rain forests. The Amazon Forest in South America is the world's largest rain forest.

DESERTS

Hot or Cold

A desert is an area where the rainfall is less than 25cm (10 ins) per year.

The polar regions are examples of cold desert areas.

The Sahara is a hot desert. Hot deserts cover about 20 per cent of the Earth's land surface.

Desert Downpour

In some deserts the year's total rainfall comes from a few heavy showers. The rains provide enough water for some plants to grow.

Desert Giants

Huge cacti grow in the American deserts. Some are 15m (50ft) tall. They store water in their thick leaves and stems.

The Driest Desert

The Atacama Desert in Chile is the driest place on Earth. In parts, no rain had fallen for 400 years, from 1570 until 1971. Other parts of this desert have never had rain.

Snow in the Desert

Winter snow falls on some of the deserts in North America.

Sometimes snow falls on the mountains in the Sahara Desert.

Temperature Changes

Hot deserts have very high daytime temperatures but at night the temperature can fall below freezing.

The Big Desert

The Sahara Desert in North Africa is the largest desert in the world. It covers almost 9 million square kilometres (3.2 million square miles).

Less than one quarter of the Sahara Desert is sand. Most of it is stone and pebbles.

The Sahara's Past

The Sahara was not always a desert. Millions of years ago it was covered in grasslands and forests.

Sandhills – Sandy Mountains

Sand dunes build up when sand is blown across the desert. The wind moves the sand dunes. Large sand dunes may be as high as 307m (1000ft) or more.

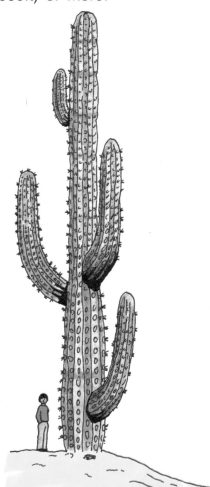

Desert Nomads

Most of the people who live in the desert are nomads. They wander from place to place in search of grass and water for their animals.

A fertile place in the desert is called an oasis. The water comes from an underground stream.

On The Move

Deserts are growing larger. The sand is spreading by as much as 61cm (2ft) a day. Scientists think it is happening because of creeping sand dunes and overgrazing of the grasses at the edges of the desert.

Oil Rich

Some of the world's largest oil fields are found in deserts. They are also rich in salt, natural gas and minerals.

TUNDRA – The Frozen Arctic Plain

The tundra lies between the Arctic polar region and the northern forests. Siberia, Norway, Finland, Sweden, Greenland and northern Canada are tundra areas. The land is frozen and covered by snow for nearly two-thirds of the year. For a short time, during the summer, about 15cm (6 inches) of the surface thaws and mosses and lichens appear. Below this the earth remains frozen.

Clever Creatures

The animals and birds which live on the tundra change colour with the seasons. To match the snow, arctic foxes, snowy owls and stoats turn white in autumn. They change back to their summer colours in spring.

EARTH'S GRASSLANDS

Grasslands are found in parts of Australia, Europe, North and South America, Asia and South Africa.

Grasslands provide food for people and animals. Grasslands can be grazed by animals or used for growing crops.

There are hundreds of different kinds of grass. Millet, rice and sugar cane are grasses. Cereal crops such as maize, wheat, barley and oats have been developed from wild grasses.

EARTH'S SAVANNAHS

Savannahs are found in South America, South East Asia and parts of Australia, where it is warm all the year round. The largest Savannahs are found in Africa. Some Savannahs get very little rain and are dry for most of the year. Others get far more rain and are dry for only three months of the year.

Ideal Home

Savannahs are large, open, grassy plains. There are patches of tall grass, clumps of small trees and scattered water holes. The large amount of food available in the Savannah attracts many grass-eating animals (herbivores).

Herds of antelope, zebra, elephant and giraffe live in the African Savannah. They provide food for the meat-eating animals (carnivores).

Leopards, lions, cheetahs and other flesh-eaters prey on the grass-eaters.

The remains of their meals are eaten by scavengers, such as vultures and hyenas.

Some animals hide in the long grass, their colour and coat markings making them difficult to see.

EARTH'S NATURAL RESOURCES

Fossil Fuels

Oil, coal and gas were formed millions of years ago under the Earth's surface. They are used to provide heat and light. Other products are made from oil and coal.

Oil Products	Coal Products
Petrol	Coal gas
Paraffin	Plastics
Paints	Antiseptics
Detergents	Perfumes
Plastics	
Cosmetics	
Pharmaceuticals	
Fuel for jet engines	
Diesel fuel	

45

Trees

Every year, large areas of forest are cut down. Nearly half of the people in the world use wood for cooking and heating.

Trees provide timber for building. Timber is used to make many other things such as furniture and matches. Wood pulp is used to make paper and plastics.

Rubber, medicine and dyes are products from rain forest trees.

The Sun

The heat from the Sun can be trapped and stored in solar panels and used to heat water.

Solar cells that absorb sunlight are used to generate electricity.

Today, solar panels are being used to provide heating and hot water to many homes in the USA, Canada, Israel, Japan and Australia.

COPPER SHEET SUN'S RAYS

HOT WATER OUT

GLASS COVER

BLACK MATERIAL TO ABSORB HEAT

COLD WATER IN

SOLAR PANEL

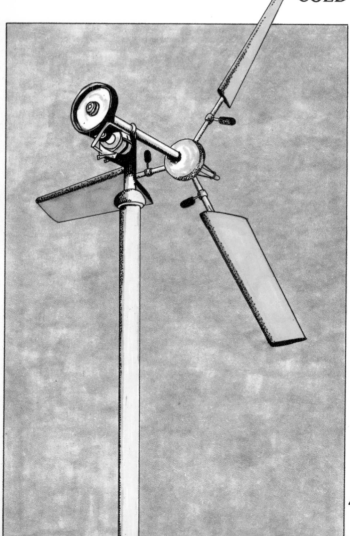

The Wind

Wind power can generate electricity. Windmills are sited where the wind blows steadily all the year round.

Water

Rivers: The flow of water in rivers and over waterfalls is used to generate electricity. Almost one quarter of the world's electricity is made by using water power.

Seas: Electricity can also be produced by using the power of the rising and falling tides. Some of the world's highest tides occur near St Malo in France. A tidal power station has been built across the estuary of the River 'Rance.

Steam Heat

In some places the hot water and steam trapped in the Earth can be piped up from under the ground and used to heat houses, office buildings and factories. Many homes in Siberia and Iceland, and parts of the USA, use this form of heating.

Rocks

The metals and minerals found in the rocks of the Earth's crust are useful to man. For example, many thousands of tonnes of bauxite are mined each year to supply the world with aluminium.

The Changing World

For hundreds of years people have been using up the Earth's natural resources.

Man has made harmful changes to the Earth. The landscape has been changed. The air and water have been polluted. People have created many problems for the future of the Earth, but are now finding better ways to live.

BAUXITE (Aluminium)

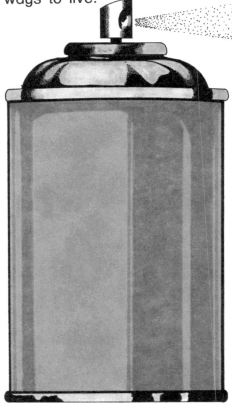

Protecting the Earth

1. Many people are trying to prevent the destruction of the rain forest. Trees take in carbon dioxide and release oxygen into the air.

2. More trees are being planted. Some of them will be used to provide fuel for cooking and heating.

3. Small trees and bushes are being planted at the edges of deserts to stop the sand from spreading over the farmland.

4. Power stations are fitted with filters to help to prevent harmful gases reaching the atmosphere.

5. Gases and factory waste can be treated in other ways instead of being dumped into the atmosphere or rivers and lakes.

6. Lead-free petrol has been developed to reduce the pollution caused by exhaust fumes.

7. Recycling

In some countries rubbish is being recycled:

a. Glass bottles and aluminium cans are melted down and re-used.

b. Cardboard and waste paper are turned into pulp which can be used to make paper products such as tissues, note-paper, toilet rolls and packaging.

c. To save coal and oil, electricity can be generated by burning rubbish.

THE EARTH'S WEATHER AND CLIMATE

There is a difference

Weather refers to the atmospheric conditions that exist in any one place and at any one time. Weather conditions can change and cause variations in the weather.

Weather is caused by combinations of different elements, such as sunshine, rainfall, wind, cloud and air pressure.

Weather happens in the troposphere – the lowest layer in the Earth's atmosphere from the Earth's surface to about 16km (10 miles) above.

No Weather – No Life It is the weather that spreads the Sun's heat around the world. Without weather, the poles would get colder and colder and the tropics would get hotter and hotter.

There would be no life on Earth.

Climate

By observing weather conditions over a long period of time meteorologists (people who study the science of the atmosphere) are able to measure the usual pattern of weather occurring at a particular place.

Climate refers to the general atmospheric conditions which 'normally' exist at a place.
Climate can be affected by winds, ocean currents and mountains.

MAIN BANDS OF CLIMATE

Cool at Poles	
Warm	
Hot at Equator	
Warm	
Cool at Poles	

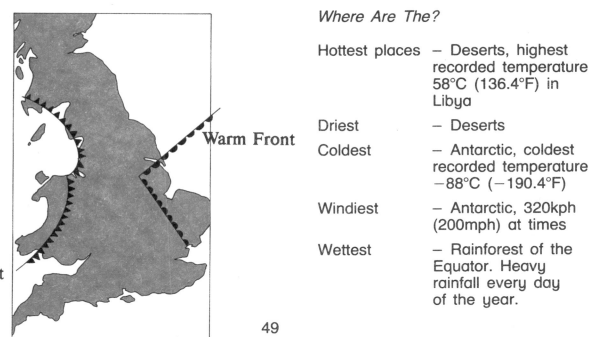

Cold Front

Warm Front

The World's Climates

There are three main bands of climate.

Tropical

Areas near to the Equator are the hottest. These are known as the Tropics.

Polar

The coldest climates are in the Arctic and the Antarctic.

Temperate

The areas between the Tropics and the Poles usually have mild winters and dry, warm summers.

Where Are The?

Hottest places	– Deserts, highest recorded temperature 58°C (136.4°F) in Libya
Driest	– Deserts
Coldest	– Antarctic, coldest recorded temperature −88°C (−190.4°F)
Windiest	– Antarctic, 320kph (200mph) at times
Wettest	– Rainforest of the Equator. Heavy rainfall every day of the year.

To Measure the Weather

Barometer – measures air pressure.

Air pressure (atmospheric pressure) is the air pressing down all over the Earth.

Air pressure varies daily from place to place and decreases the higher up you go. Aeroplanes are pressurised so people can breathe at high altitudes.

Thermometer – measures temperature (degrees of heat or coldness). Invented by Galileo Galilei in 1607.

Thermograph – used to give a continuous record of air temperature, traced on a strip of paper called a thermogram.

Rain Gauge – a device with a funnel to collect and measure the amount of rainfall in one day.

Measuring Clouds

Cloud cover is measured in 'oktas' or eighths of the sky. 0 oktas means a clear sky, 8 oktas means that the sky is totally covered in cloud.

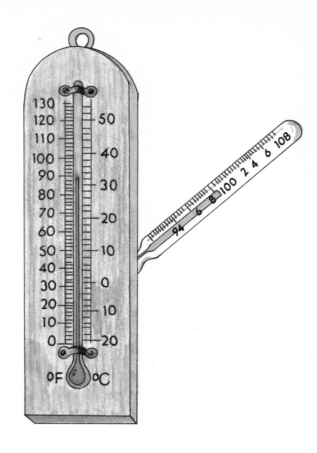

Sunshine

Sunshine is measured with a 'sunshine recorder'. This is a glass ball which focuses the Sun's rays onto a strip of paper. As the Sun crosses the sky the heat from it, when it is not obscured by cloud, burns a mark on the paper which shows the hours of sunshine in a day.

Wind

Anemometers measure wind speed. A windsock or wind vane shows direction. The 'Beaufort' scale, invented by Admiral Beaufort in 1805, is used to describe wind strength and wind speed. On the Beaufort scale, 2–6 = breezes, 7–10 = gales, 11 = storms, 12 = hurricane.

Radiosonde Balloon

A large balloon used to carry instruments up into the atmosphere to radio data back to the ground.

Weather Satellites

Some satellites are made to travel at the same speed at which the Earth is rotating and they therefore stay above the same place on Earth. These are called geo-stationary satellites and orbit about 35,000km (22,000 miles) above the Equator.

Polar orbiting satellites pass over the Poles and the Equator.

Satellites send back to Earth photographs of cloud positions.

Wet and Dry Bulb Thermometer

Used to measure humidity (the amount of water vapour in the air).

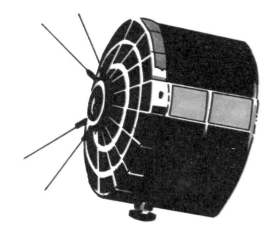

TIROS I USA

Weather satellite

ALL KINDS OF WEATHER

Sunshine

The Sun's rays filter through the atmosphere and warm the surface of the Earth. The heat rises from the Earth's surface and is trapped in the atmosphere. The amount of sunlight reaching the Earth keeps most of the surface temperature suitable for nearly all living things.

IF less sunlight reached the Earth it would cause an Ice Age. The oceans would freeze and no life would be possible on Earth.

Ice Ages

Over the centuries, the Earth's climate slowly changes. There are cold glacial periods known as Ice Ages and warm interglacial periods. We are living in an interglacial which began about 10,000 years ago.

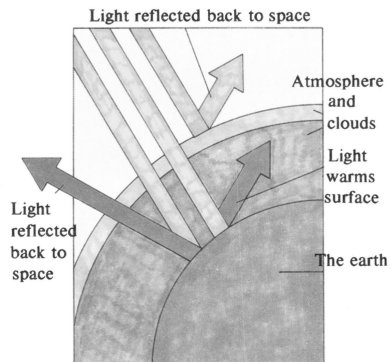

Light reflected back to space

Atmosphere and clouds

Light warms surface

Light reflected back to space

The earth

Cloud

Clouds are formed when warm air rises and the water vapour cools down sufficiently to become water droplets.

There are three main types —

1. Cirrus — often a sign of bad weather.
2. Cumulus — often a sign of sunny weather.
3. Stratus — often a sign of drizzling rain.

Fog

Fog is really cloud formed at low level.

Sea fogs occur when warm air from the land spreads over the cold seas.

Drizzle and Rain

Tiny drops of rain are called drizzle. Raindrops come from clouds. Water droplets join together until they form a raindrop heavy enough to fall.

Too much rain can bring flooding which can cause great damage and loss of life.

▲ 1

▲ 2

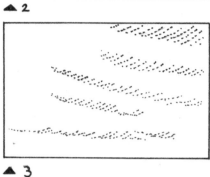

▲ 3

A SNOWFLAKE

Drought

Lack of rain causes droughts. Few plants can survive drought conditions and this causes famines in some parts of the world.

Frost

If the temperature falls below freezing a frost occurs and water turns to ice. Water expands when it freezes and can cause water pipes to burst. Ice floats on water.

Snow

Snowflakes form from frozen water vapour. Every snowflake has six sides and every one has a different pattern.

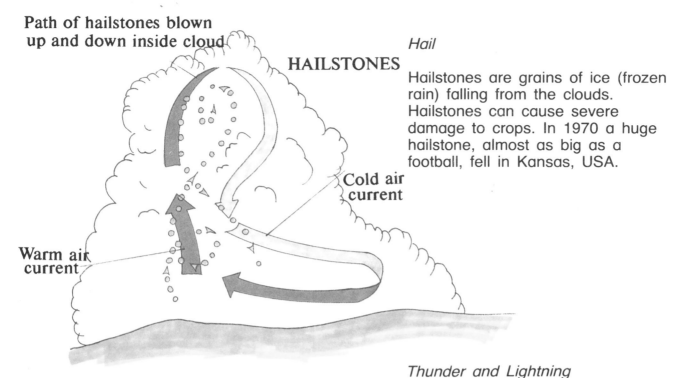

Path of hailstones blown up and down inside cloud

HAILSTONES

Cold air current

Warm air current

Hail

Hailstones are grains of ice (frozen rain) falling from the clouds. Hailstones can cause severe damage to crops. In 1970 a huge hailstone, almost as big as a football, fell in Kansas, USA.

Thunder and Lightning

A thunderstorm is one of the most dramatic events that occurs in the atmosphere. Storms are more likely to happen when the air is warm and humid and usually last for one or two hours. They begin when large cumulus clouds (thunder clouds) form in the sky.

Lightning flashes are caused by the electricity which builds up in a thunder cloud. Lightning can travel from cloud to cloud as well as to the ground.

The noise of thunder is caused by the rapid expansion of the air heated by the flash of lightning to a temperature five times hotter than that of the Sun.

Thunder and lightning happen at the same time but because light travels faster than sound we see the lightning before we hear the thunder when we are some distance from the storm.

A Very Noisy Place ...

Bogor in Java has had as many as 322 thundery days in one year. It usually has about 215 days when thunderstorms occur.

... in a Noisy World

The world has about sixteen million thunderstorms each year.

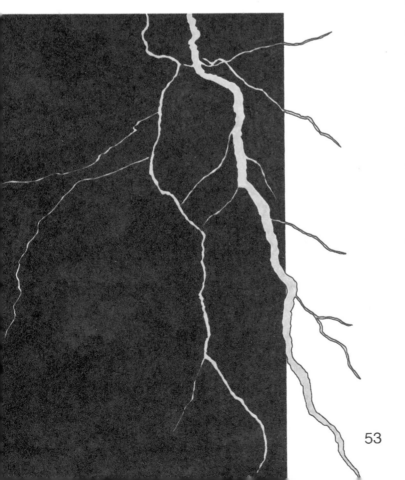

Major Wind

Wind is moving air caused by differences in temperature and air pressure.

Winds blow from high to low pressure areas. The Equator is a low pressure area and the Poles are high pressure areas.

Due to the West–East rotation of the Earth, winds in the northern hemisphere swing to the right and winds in the southern hemisphere swing to the left. This is known as the Coriolis effect.

Wind Names

The Mistral — the cold NW wind that can blow over Southern France.

The Levanter — the violent E wind that can blow in the Eastern Mediterranean.

The Chinook — the warm, dry wind blowing down the Eastern side of the Rocky Mountains in the USA.

WORLD WINDS

POLAR EASTERLIES

WESTERLIES

TRADES

TRADES

WESTERLIES

POLAR EASTERLIES

EQUATOR

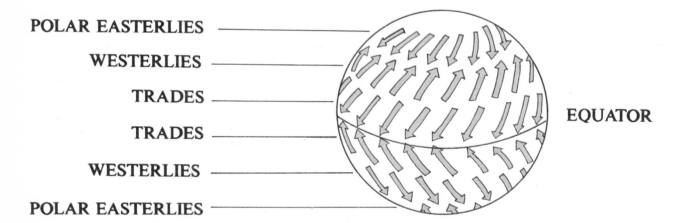

Hurricane Horror

Wind, rain and storm clouds whirl round in these violent and powerful West Indian tropical storms at up to 300km/h (190mph). They begin over warm seas and can be up to 500km (310 miles) in diameter. They can start to die down when they reach land.

The centre of a hurricane, the 'eye', has calm weather. It is about 32km (20 miles across). Hurricanes are given names. In 1979 Dominica, in the West Indies, was hit by Hurricane David. Two thousand people died and 20,000 were left homeless.

Any wind in the world of more than 120km/h (75mph) is said to be 'of hurricane force'.

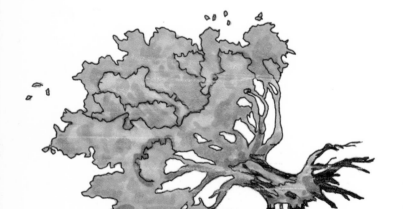

Tornado Terror

A tornado is a very violent whirling wind storm which travels across a narrow strip of countryside. It is very much smaller than a hurricane but can do a tremendous amount of damage in a small area. Black funnel-shaped storm clouds twist violently, sucking up anything in their path.

Rainbows in the Sky

When sunlight passes through drops of water a rainbow appears. White sunlight breaks up into its colours — red, orange, yellow, green, blue, indigo and violet.

Changing Seasons

The Earth moving round the Sun causes the changes in the seasons. More sunlight and heat reach different parts and at different times.

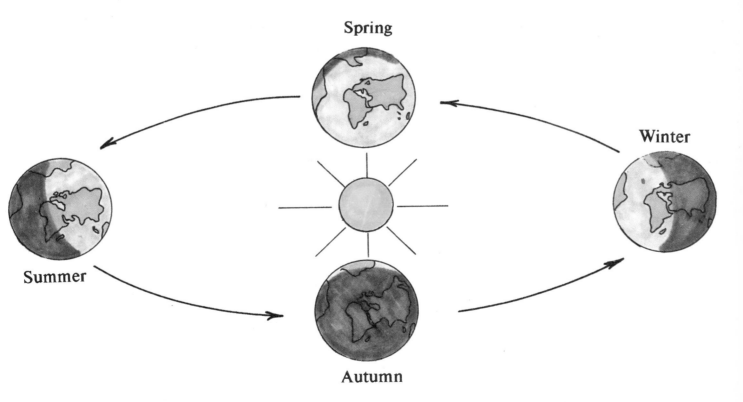

Spring

Winter

Summer

Autumn

55

PEOPLE

Man has existed on Earth for a tiny fraction of time since the Earth was 'born'.

If we were to imagine that life on Earth had existed for only one day, then man's stay on Earth would occupy only a few seconds.

But, during his comparatively short time on Earth, man has made enormous advances. He has established his superiority over the rest of the animal kingdom, his numbers have increased dramatically and he has organised himself into groups, tribes or nations.

The Appearance of Man

The earliest traces of human life were found in Africa.

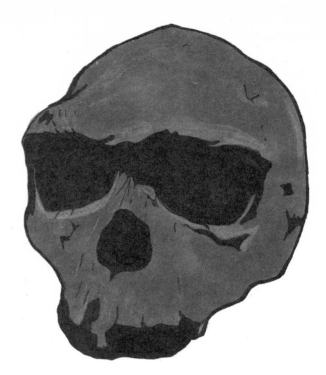

HUMAN FOSSIL

The World's Oldest 'Human' Footprint

Footprints made $3\frac{3}{4}$ million years ago by man-like apes, our earliest human ancestors, were discovered in Tanzania in 1978.

The First Human Beings

It is at least two million years since the first true human beings existed on Earth. They were named Homo habilis (Latin for able man) because they made the first known tools.

Fossil Evidence

Human fossils have been found in many parts of the world. Fossils provide information about life on Earth in prehistoric times. Prehistoric = before written records began.

A Special Skeleton

The Neanderthal skeleton was discovered in Germany in 1856 and named after the river by which it was found.

The skeleton belonged to an earlier type of man who had lived on Earth between 40,000 and 200,000 years ago. Since the discovery of the Neanderthal skeleton, people have believed that our ancestors were apes.

People who study the evolution of human beings are called anthropologists.

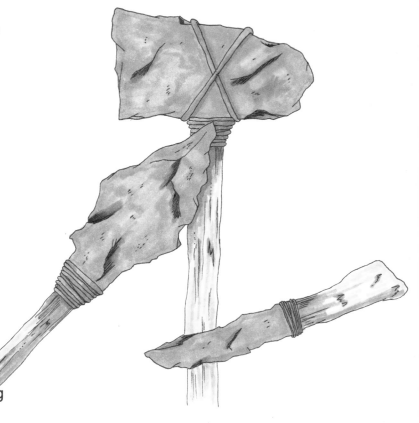

The Earth's People

All the people alive today belong to the species Homo sapiens (Modern Man).

Early Man

Early men found food by gathering nuts, fruit and berries and by hunting and trapping wild animals. They were hunter-gatherers.

They learned to make rough tools and simple weapons from bone, wood and stone. The first tools were stones with sharp edges.

CAVE DRAWINGS

These early people did not stay in one place but moved about, following the wild animals they hunted. At first they wrapped themselves in skins taken from the animals they killed. Later they learned how to sew the skins together to make clothes.

Siberian Surprise!

A clothed body, believed to be at least 37,000 years old, was found in Siberia's frozen ground. The trousers and shirt were made from animal skins.

Fire! Fire!

The first fires may have been started by lightning.

Early man learned how to control fire and, at first, used it for keeping warm and later for cooking food.

As time passed, man began to make more efficient tools and weapons. Bows and arrows were used and people still lived by hunting and gathering food.

Bones were used to make combs and needles. Animal tendons and plant fibres were used as thread.

Dramatic Developments
(about 10,000 years ago)

First Farmers

By this time people had begun to live in villages. They had learned to *produce* their food by growing seeds from wild plants such as wheat and barley. They made bread. Animals such as dogs, sheep, goats, cattle and pigs became domesticated. Man used the animals to provide meat and milk and he also used the skins and wool.

The plough was invented, a simple device, made from the branches of trees and dragged by men.

Civilisation Begins

The coming of agriculture increased the supply of food, more people survived and the population grew.

To prevent other tribes from stealing their food and animals, people built walls around their settlements. These were the beginnings of the first cities. The city-dwellers (citizens) began to trade their products.

This brought about a new way of life which we call *civilisation*.

THE AMAZING HUMAN BODY

A Marvellous Machine

A skeleton holds the body together. The 650 different muscles covering the skeleton give the body its shape.

Babies have 305 bones at birth. Adults have about 206 bones because as people grow some of the bones fuse together.

There are more than 100 joints in a human skeleton.

A human being breathes about 500 million times in an average lifetime and the heart will beat about 3,000 million times.

The heart pumps blood around 96,000 km (59,654 miles) of arteries, veins and capillaries at a rate of 5½ litres (9.7pts) per minute.

An adult body contains between 3½ and 6 litres (6.2 and 10.6pts) of blood.

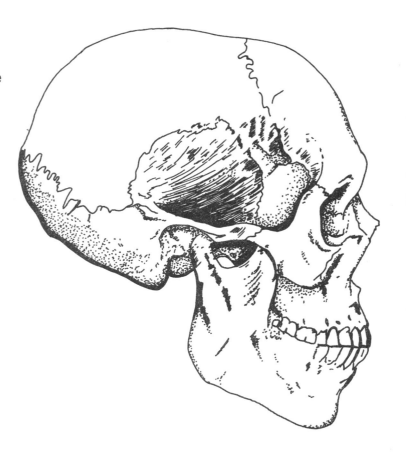

The body is made up of millions of cells. Some, such as bone cells, last for years; others live for only a few days.

Red blood cells carry oxygen. White blood cells fight disease.

Body Fuel

In a lifetime an average person eats 50 tonnes of food and drinks 42,000 litres (9,240 galls) of liquid.

Everybody has about 9 metres (29.5ft) of intestine coiled up inside them.

59

The tongue has about 9,500 taste buds.

Birthday Suit

A waterproof skin covers the human body. Skin wears away and is replaced every few weeks. About 70% of the body is water.

One square centimetre (⅙sq in) of skin has about 100 sweat glands which release salty water to evaporate and cool the body. As much as a ¼ litre (0.44pt) of water a day is lost from the body as sweat.

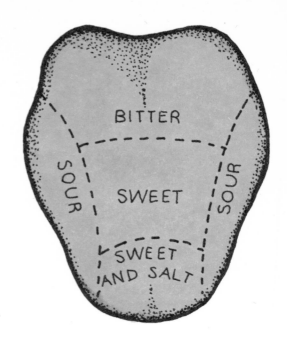

A "TASTE MAP"
OF THE TONGUE

Sensitive Suit

A body has about 13 million nerve cells. Nerve endings help us to feel. We are able to experience pain or comfort and detect heat and cold.

In Control

The human brain controls everything we do. The brain's messages travel through the nervous system.

Did You Know?

There is enough fat in a human body to make seven bars of soap.

There is also as much iron as there is in a 2½ cm (1in) nail.

Normal body temperature is 37°C.

No two people have exactly the same fingerprints.

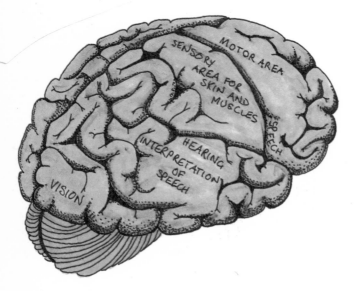

THE HUMAN BRAIN

POPULATION

People in the World

In 1990 the world population was over 5,000 million.

Every day it increases by more than 200,000. It is thought that by the end of this century the world population will have almost doubled.

The Four Largest Populations

1st China, with more than one thousand million people
2nd India
3rd USSR
4th USA

Languages

There are now over 5,000 different languages and dialects spoken in the world.

The most spoken language is Chinese; the second is English.

English is the most used language; nearly one third of the world's people speak English.

In the 1880s an international language called Esperanto (hope) was invented by Ludwik Zamenhof. He hoped his new language would bring peace and understanding throughout the world.

People and Clothes

Man's first clothes were animal skins.

About 6000 BC. A Most Important Discovery

Weaving – probably began when reeds and canes were used to make baskets.

Man learned how to obtain plant and animal fibres such as flax, cotton and wool. These were woven into cloth (textiles). Textiles have been used for clothing ever since. People wear clothes which are suitable for the climate in which they live. For example, people who live in cold places wear fur to keep themselves warm. People who live in hot places wear long, loose robes to keep themselves cool.

People and Food

Food fuels and maintains our bodies.

The Right Balance

To keep healthy our bodies need a supply of carbohydrates, fats, proteins, minerals and vitamins.

People need a balance of different kinds of food such as meat, fish, milk, cereals, eggs, fruit and vegetables.

Calorie Count

Food energy is measured in calories. To stay healthy we need 3,000 to 3,500 calories a day.

In parts of Africa and Asia many people live on a poor diet which does not provide the food energy they need.

Feeding the World

There is a world-wide trade in food supplies. Different parts of the world are suited to growing different crops and making different products.

Who Grows Most?

Potatoes:	USSR, China, Poland, USA
Bananas:	Brazil, Ecuador, Mexico
Tea:	India, China, Sri Lanka
Grapes:	Italy, France, Spain
Rice:	China
Maize:	USA
Soya Beans:	USA
Wheat:	USSR
Barley:	USSR

Who Produces Most?

Beef:	USA, USSR, Argentina, EEC
Milk:	USSR, USA, France
Wine:	Italy, France, Spain
Sugar:	Brazil, USSR, Cuba
Coffee:	Brazil, Colombia, Indonesia
Beer:	USA, Germany, USSR, Great Britain

Sheep Farming

Australia, New Zealand

Fishing

Japan, USSR, China, USA

Food For The Future

Scientists are finding new food resources to meet the growing demand. For example, ocean fish farming, plant farming in the sea and the use of genetic engineering. It is now possible to breed sheep which provide more wool, pigs and cattle which produce more meat and plants that produce greater yields.

A type of seaweed called the giant kelp could become an important food source for human beings. At the moment it is used only for cattle food.

People: Sports and Pastimes

The Olympic Games

The first Ancient Olympic Games were held in 776 BC in Greece. They were held every four years until 394 AD.

It is thought that competitive games had been held long before.

The Modern Olympic Games were revived at Athens in 1896. They have taken place every four years since, except during the two World Wars.

The Olympic Torch

The Olympic Torch is lit by the sun's rays at Olympia (Greece). Relays of runners carry the torch to wherever the Games are being held.

A Few Facts

a. The modern trampoline was invented in the 1940s by an American called George Nissen.

b. Water Polo was invented about 100 years ago. It was originally called 'Football in the Water'.

c. Toboganning dates from the 16th century. It became established as a racing sport in Switzerland in about 1879.

Lying on your back going down the course feet first is called luge toboganning. Lying on your front going down the course head first is called skeleton toboganning.

d. Wrestling is one of the oldest known sports. There are various styles of wrestling such as Sumo in Japan and Kushti in Iran.

e. Karate became popular in Japan in the 1920s. Karate means 'empty hand'.

f. In 1875 Captain Matthew Webb became the first person to swim the English Channel.

g. For thousands of years people have been fascinated by feats of strength. Weightlifting competitions were held in the Ancient Olympic Games. Today, competitors in the Super Heavyweight class are required to lift more than 110 kg (242½lbs).

h. Harness Racing dates from the chariot races of 3,000 years ago.

i. Roger Bannister (Great Britain) was the first athlete to run a mile in less than four minutes. In 1954 he ran a mile in 3 min. 59.4 secs.

j. Soccer is the world's most popular sport. More people play and watch soccer than any other sport. The World Cup Competition is held every four years. The winners are awarded the Jules Rimet Trophy.

k. A type of ski was used around 3,000 BC as a means of transport.

l. The game of Rugby was first played in 1823 at Rugby School (England) when William Webb Ellis picked up the ball and ran with it during a game of football.

m. Ice Hockey is the world's fastest team game.

THE ARTS AND ENTERTAINMENT

The World's Oldest Paintings

The oldest paintings date from prehistoric times. Pictures of animals such as mammoths, bison and deer have been found on cave walls. The cave paintings at Lascaux, in France, are about 30,000 years old.

The 'Mona Lisa'

The famous 'Mona Lisa', painted by Leonardo da Vinci in 1507, is probably the most valuable painting in the world. It hangs in the Louvre Museum in Paris, France.

Modern Art

The Spanish painter Pablo Picasso (1881–1973) was one of the most famous artists of modern times.

Modern artists have made sculptures from scrap metal and used tyres.

A huge orange curtain hung across the Grand Canyon, USA, (1970–72) has been described as art.

Writing

Writing began about 5,500 years ago. At first people scratched 'word' pictures on pieces of clay which were then dried.

Writers in some countries, such as Egypt and China, began to use symbols. For example, an eye meant 'see'.

CAVE DRAWINGS

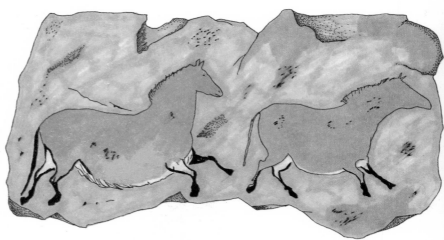

Later, writers used wedge-shaped signs to express words, ideas and actions and thus a more organised form of writing existed.

The Rosetta Stone

The Rosetta Stone dates from about 196 BC. It was one of the most important discoveries. On it is carved an inscription in hieroglyphics and letters. By comparing both kinds of writing it became possible to read the meaning of the hieroglyphics.

THE ROSETTA STONE

Braille Writing

Blind people can 'read' by using Braille writing: a system of raised dots arranged to represent the letters of the alphabet and numbers. It was devised in 1829 by the French inventor Louis Braille.

The Bible

The Bible has been translated into more than 300 languages.

Shakespeare

William Shakespeare (1564–1616) was one of the world's greatest playwrights. His 37 plays include *Macbeth, Romeo and Juliet, King Lear* and *Hamlet*, his longest play with 4042 lines.

Millions of Books

The United States Library of Congress contains more than 86 million items. It is the largest library in the world.

shakespeare

First published in 1955, 'The Guinness Book of Records' has sold more than 50 million copies world wide.

Music

From the beginning Man made music with his voice and by clapping his hands and stamping his feet. Drums were made from animal skins stretched over hollow logs. Percussion instruments were probably the first musical instruments to come into existence.

Famous Composers

Johann Sebastian Bach (1685–1750) is best known for his church and organ music.

Wolfgang Amadeus Mozart (1756–91) is thought to be one of the world's greatest composers. He began writing music at the age of four and his best-known works are symphonies and operas.

mozart

Ludwig van Beethoven (1770–1827) is best known for his symphonies and chamber music.

Johannes Brahms (1833–97) is famous for his music composed for voice and piano and also his choral music.

Peter Ilyitch Tchaikovsky (1840–93). One of his best-known works is the Festival Overture written in 1880 to commemorate Napoleon's retreat from Moscow in 1812.

Famous Opera Houses

La Scala, Milan, Italy. The interior is horseshoe shaped. There are five tiers of boxes, 194 in all, and a gallery above. It can hold an audience of 3,600.

The Metropolitan, New York, USA. The 'Met' was opened in 1883. It has seats for 3,500 people and standing room for 600 more.

The Paris Opéra, Paris, France. The building, which is 80m (262ft) high and 173m (568ft) long, can hold 2,600 people.

beethoven

Pop Music

The Beatles sold more than one thousand million tapes and records. They were the most successful pop group in the world.

Band Aid. In 1985, on July 13th, two pop concerts were held, one in London and one in Philadelphia. The money raised was used to help starving people in Africa.

Best Seller

The best-selling record ever is Irving Berlin's *White Christmas*. It was recorded in 1942 by the American singer Bing Crosby and more than 170 million copies have been sold.

For the Record

The gramophone was invented in 1877, the tape recorder in 1935, the transistor radio in 1948 and stereo recording in 1958.

Ballet

Anna Pavlova (1882–1931) was the idol of ballet-lovers in every country and is said to have been the greatest ballerina of all time.

The Russian dancer Vaslav Nijinsky (1890–1950) was known as 'The God of Dance'. He and Anna Pavlova danced for Serge Diaghilev's Russian Ballet.

Did You Know?

A balletomane is an enthusiastic ballet 'fan': someone who is ballet 'mad'.

Film

Film-making was invented by the French brothers Lumière less than 100 years ago.

The first films were silent pictures accompanied by a pianist or an orchestra.

'The Jazz Singer' made in 1927 was the first feature film with voices, sounds and music to go along with the pictures.

'Star Trek' was one of the most expensive films ever made. It cost 21 million US dollars.

TV and Radio

Television was first demonstrated in 1924 by the Scottish inventor John Logie Baird.

In 1936 television broadcasting was begun by the BBC (British Broadcasting Corporation).

Telstar was the world's first communications satellite. It was launched in 1962.

Using satellites orbiting the earth, television pictures can be beamed live between continents. It is possible for an event, like the World Cup, to be seen by an audience of more than two billion people.

Television sets can be made small enough to be worn on the wrist like a watch.

MARCONI

Guglielmo Marconi (1874–1937) sent the first radio signals from England on December 12th 1901. The signals were received in Newfoundland, Canada.

The transistor radio was invented in 1948 but it was 1953 before transistors came into general use.

The Morse Code was invented in 1838 by the American Samuel Morse.

The international distress call is three dots, three dashes, three dots

. . .   — — —   . . .

S   O   S

THE NATURAL WORLD

Earth's history is one of endless change. This is particularly true of plant and animal life.

Evolution is the story of the way living things have changed since life began.

In the Beginning

First Life

The Earth's first living cells floated in water 3,200 million years ago.

First Plants

Simple plant life, called blue-green algae, began to form about 3,000 million years ago.

Plants lived on Earth long before the first animals. Plants produce oxygen which animals breathe to stay alive. Animals depend on plants for their food.

A LIZARD FEEDING

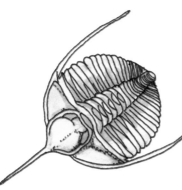

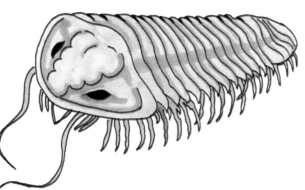

TRILOBITES

First Animals

Fossils of worms, and jellyfish, the first known animals, were found in Australia. They are about 670 million years old.

Trilobites appeared 570 million years ago. They were the first animals to have eyes. Trilobites are the ancestors of today's lobsters and shrimps.

The first known shellfish appeared 570–500 million years ago. Some shellfish could swim because their shells contained chambers of water and gas. They were called Nautiloids.

A huge variety of shellfish called Ammonites lived between 230 and 65 million years ago. Some shells were as much as 2m (6½ft) in diameter.

The First Fish

The first fish appeared on Earth about 500 million years ago. They were called Ostracoderms.

Fish were the *first vertebrates* (animals with backbones). They had no jaws but sucked in particles of food from the muddy sea bed.
By 395 million years ago (The Devonian Period) fish called Placoderms lived on Earth. They had developed jaws, which meant that they had a wider choice of food. Because so many new species of fish developed, this period of Earth's history is also known as 'The Age of the Fish'.

Amphibians

The first amphibians (animals that are able to live on land and in water) lived about 350 million years ago. Fossil evidence shows that they looked like giant salamanders with long heads and well-developed tails.

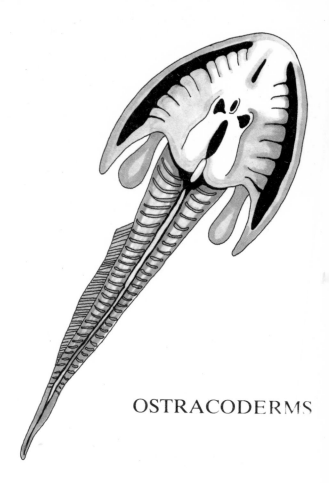

OSTRACODERMS

Groups of amphibians exist today. There are more than 2,500 species of frogs and toads and about 225 species of newts and salamanders.

Reptiles appeared on Earth about 300 million years ago. Unlike their ancestors, the early amphibians, reptiles could live entirely on land. The hard-shelled egg had evolved which meant that fully-developed, but tiny, adults hatched.

Thecodants were reptiles that stood on their hind legs, leaving the fore limbs free for grasping. As time passed, they were to evolve into some of the largest animals ever to live on the Earth — the dinosaurs.

A PREHISTORIC REPTILE

The Age of Dinosaurs

Dinosaurs were reptiles that lived on Earth from about 225 to 65 million years ago. No-one knows why they died out. Dinosaur fossils have been found all over the world. Dinosaur means 'terrible lizard'.

The largest animals ever to have lived on land were Sauropods, plant-eating dinosaurs.

Diplodocus was 25m (82ft) long and weighed 11 tonnes.

Brontosaurus was 21m (68ft) long and weighed 30 tonnes.

Brachiosaurus was 28m (91ft) long and weighed 100 tonnes.

Most dinosaurs had very small brains.

BRONTOSAURUS

Some plant-eating (herbivorous) dinosaurs had bony plates and scales to protect them from the meat-eating dinosaurs. Stegosaurus and Ankylosaurus were both heavily armoured.

Horned dinosaurs, such as Torosaurus, had frills of bone to protect their necks.

Triceratops had horns that were nearly 1m (3ft) long. It was one of the last dinosaurs on Earth.

Hadrosaurs were among the most common dinosaurs. They lived about 85–65 million years ago. They had more than 2,000 teeth. As the teeth wore out new ones grew.

There were giant meat-eating dinosaurs.

Teratosaurus was 6m (19ft) long and weighed 7 tonnes.

Megalosaurus was 9m (30ft) long and weighed 9 tonnes.

TOROSAURUS

The fiercest of all was Tyrannosaurus Rex. It was 5½m (18ft) tall, 12m (39ft) long and weighed 6½ tonnes. Its teeth were 18cm (7″) long.

Not all dinosaurs were huge and slow-moving. A dinosaur named Saltopus, found in Scotland (UK), was only 60cm (2ft) long. The Gallimimus ran on long thin hind legs and probably reached speeds of 56kph (35mph), almost as fast as a galloping horse.

Prehistoric Flying Animals

Insects appeared on the Earth about 300 million years ago. They were the first animals to fly. Today there are more than a million species of insects. They are the most numerous of all living creatures.

Pterosaurs (flying reptiles) lived between 195–65 million years ago. The Quetzalcoatlus, with a wing span of 12m (39ft), is believed to be the largest animal ever to have flown.

TYRANNOSAURUS REX

The first true bird was probably Hesperornis, a huge, 2m (6ft) long sea bird that could not fly. It lived about 80 million years ago.

Prehistoric Mammals

Mammals are warm-blooded animals which have hair or fur and they feed their young with their own milk.

Mammals developed from mammal-like reptiles about 190 million years ago.

The first mammals were about 10cm (4ins) in length and shrew-like in appearance.

Marsupials are a group of mammals that carry their young in pouches. Diprotodon was a prehistoric wombat as large as a grizzly bear. Procoptodon was a giant kangaroo.

DIPROTODON

The earliest known rhinoceros was a dog-sized creature which developed into Baluchitherium, the largest land animal ever to have lived. It was 5m (16ft) tall.

The first horses appeared on Earth about 55 million years ago. They had toes and were the size of cats. They developed hooves about 5 million years ago.

Smilodon, the sabre-toothed cat, was as big as a lion and had long, stabbing teeth.

Mammoths lived on Earth from 5 million years ago until about 10,000 years ago. Many perfectly-preserved animals have been found in Siberia's frozen ground.

A MAMMOTH

Present Life on Earth

Today there are about 5 million species of plants and animals living on Earth.

Creatures of the Sea and Shore

There are more fish than all other vertebrates. There are also more species of fish; at least 23,000 of them.

Fish Life

Some fish live in sea water and some in fresh. Some live deep down in the water while others swim near the surface. Some fish feed on plankton or seaweed and some on other fish or even land animals.

All fish breathe through gills. Most fish lay eggs. A cod can produce 8 million eggs at a time; a herring probably about 50,000.

Fast and Fearsome

Sharks are streamlined. They are fast swimmers and have large mouths and sharp teeth. The great white shark is the fiercest man-eating shark.

SOME SHARKS

75

'Catfish' belong to a large group of freshwater fish which are slow-moving and have barbels growing out of their mouths.

Puffed Up

Puffer fish are able to blow themselves up in size when danger threatens.

The Unusual Seahorse

The seahorse is related to the stickleback. It can swim only in an upright position and is able to cling to seaweed by its tail. The eggs are looked after by the male who carries them in a pouch in his belly until they hatch.

Clever Cuttlefish

The cuttlefish lives on the sea bottom. It is able to blow jets of water to uncover the shrimps on which it feeds. It can also bury itself in the sand.

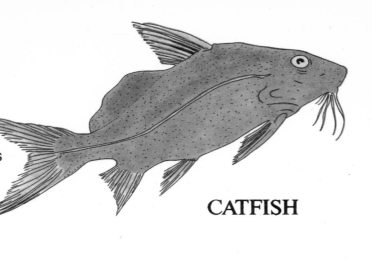

CATFISH

EEL

Electric Fish

Electric fish, such as the electric eel of South America, can stun their prey with charges of up to 500 volts.

Jellyfish

Many species of jellyfish float in the world's oceans. The Portuguese Man o' War can grow tentacles up to 18 m (58ft) in length.

The sea wasps of the tropical Pacific are some of the most dangerous. Their poisonous sting can kill a person in less than ten minutes.

THE PORTUGUESE MAN o' WAR

JELLYFISH

Octopus and Squid

Octopuses and squids are related to clams, mussels and snails. The octopus has 8 tentacles around its mouth and the squid has 10. They both squirt out clouds of 'ink' when threatened by an enemy.

Some octopuses reach a length of 9m (29ft). The giant squid grows up to 20m (65ft) long and is the largest of all molluscs (soft-bodied creatures).

Molluscs

There are more than 80,000 known species of molluscs, many of which have shells. Giant clams can weigh more than 225kg (500lb).

Crustaceans

There are more than 30,000 species of crustaceans, which include lobsters, barnacles, shrimps, crabs and water fleas.

AN OCTOPUS

BRIGHTLY COLOURED FISH

The luminous prawn is just one of the many crustaceans capable of producing light. Hermit crabs use the abandoned shells of sea snails as their homes.

Bath Time

The bath sponge lives in the warm waters of the Caribbean and Mediterranean seas.

Coral Reefs

Reef building corals grow only in tropical oceans. The Great Barrier Reef off the coast of Australia is home to millions of shellfish and a host of brightly-coloured fish. It has been estimated that there are more than 3,000 species of animals living there.

Whales

The whales are a group of marine animals that includes all the smaller species such as dolphins and porpoises.

Whales are among the most intelligent animals that have ever lived.

Whales are the only mammals that live in water for the whole of their lives. They can hold their breath for a long time, some of them for as much as two hours.

Whales are born tail first so that they do not drown during birth. The female floats on her side to feed her baby.

The largest animal on earth is the blue whale which may be 30m (97ft) long and can weigh up to 112 tonnes. It feeds on krill (small shrimp-like animals) and can eat as much as four tonnes a day.

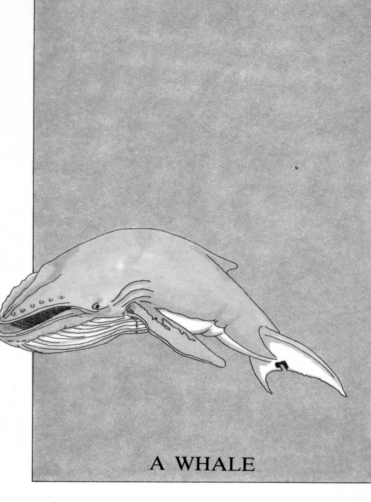

A WHALE

SOME FROGS

Amphibians

Amphibians must keep their skins moist in order to breathe. Most amphibians live in the tropics where the climate is hot and wet, but they are also found in grasslands and even deserts.

Frogs and toads go through a complete change of form during their lives. This is known as metamorphosis.

Weather Forecasting Frog

The European green tree frog changes from bright green to grey when it is frightened or when the sky is overcast. Some people keep caged frogs to forecast rain.

78

Reptiles

Turtles and crocodiles have remained unchanged since they first appeared on Earth in prehistoric times.

They are 'living fossils'.

There are 25 species of crocodiles, 3,000 of lizards, 2,800 of snakes and 250 species of turtles and tortoises.

The anaconda is the heaviest snake.

The longest reptile was a python that measured 10m (32ft).

Leatherback sea turtles can be more than 2m (6½ft) long.

A TURTLE

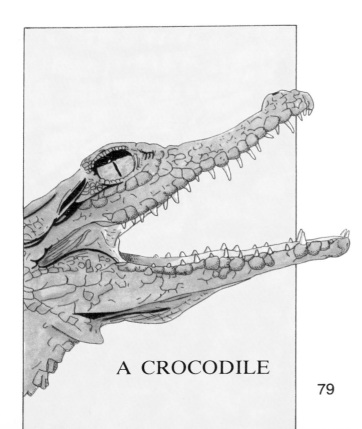

A CROCODILE

The boa constrictor is a snake that entwines a victim in its coils and squeezes until the victim suffocates.

The frilled lizard of Australia runs on its hind legs with its frill erect, to confuse and frighten an enemy.

A chameleon can flick its tongue out in 1/25th of a second. It can also change the colour of its skin to match its background.

The world's largest lizard, the Komodo dragon of Indonesia, can be up to 3m (10ft) in length.

Some crocodiles can be up to 6m (20ft) long.

Plants of the World

Plants are grouped into families, the non-flowering plants and the angiosperms which have flowers and enclosed seeds.

There are more than 400,000 known species of plants and, of these, at least 250,000 are flowering plants.

Flowering plants first appeared about 150 million years ago. The Magnolia tree was the first plant to produce flowers.

The Vascular System

To live on land plants needed a means of carrying water up from the roots and foodstuffs down from the leaves. They developed a network of woody tubes which also stiffened the plants so that they could stand upright.

A MAGNOLIA PLANT

First Land Plants

The first known land plants lived about 380 million years ago. Detailed fossils found in Rhynie, Scotland (UK) show that the plant grew to a height of 1m (39ins).

The Largest Plants

The largest plants in the world are the giant redwood trees of North America. Sequoias can grow to 107m (350ft) or more in height and may be up to $7\frac{1}{2}$m (26ft) across. They can weigh more than nine times as much as the blue whale, the heaviest animal that has ever lived.

The Smallest Flower

The Brazilian duckweed, or wolffia, has the smallest flower, less than one millimetre in diameter.

The Oldest Tree

The bristlecone pine is the world's oldest tree. Some are nearly 5,000 years old, about the same age as the Great Pyramid in Egypt.

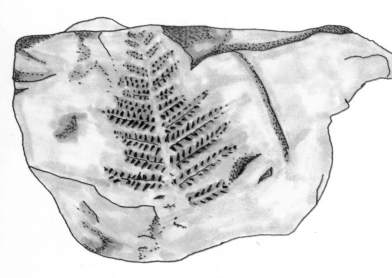

A FOSSIL

Vital to Life

Plants are the only living things that can make their own food. Green plants take in carbon dioxide gas (from the atmosphere) and water (from the earth) and using energy from the sunlight turn them into foodstuffs.

With no plants there would be nothing to feed the plant-eating animals (herbivores) which are eaten by the carnivores (meat-eaters). There are nearly three times as many plant species as there are animal species.

More than 90% of all species of flowers in the world have no smell at all.

The Rafflesia Arnoldi, of Sumatra, has the largest blossom in the world measuring 1m (3ft) across. It also gives off an overpowering stench of rotting carrion.

The truffle, a black fungus which grows underground in France and Italy, is the most costly single food and is used to flavour sauces. Farmers train pigs to root out the truffles.

The hurricane-plant is protected from being destroyed by winds by the holes in its leaves.

The Tomato – Fruit or Vegetable?

Strangely enough, the tomato is classed as a fruit by botanists because it contains seeds. It is regarded as a berry, like the raspberry or strawberry. When tomatoes were first introduced into Europe from Peru they were called 'love apples'.

Some other foods we use as vegetables are regarded as fruits – runner beans and cucumbers for example.

You probably think that the tulip originated in Holland but the flower actually came from Turkey. The word tulip comes from a Turkish word meaning turban.

During the seventeenth century when tulips first reached Europe, a Dutchman exchanged all the following for only ONE tulip bulb: 2 loads of wheat, 4 loads of rye, 4 fat oxen, 8 fat pigs, 12 fat sheep, 2 hogsheads of wine, 4 barrels of beer, 2 barrels of butter, $454\frac{1}{2}$kg (1,000lbs) of cheese, a bed, a suit of clothes and a silver beaker.

Large and Little

The bamboo which grows on the Malay Peninsula and reaches a height of 33m (120ft) is really a species of grass and is known as 'The King of Grasses'. It is the fastest-growing grass and can grow a metre a day.

There is a tiny, tiny Indian plant called an 'artillery' and it would take 72 to fill a space of $2\frac{1}{2}$cm (1ins).

The world's rarest plant is a type of silversword which is only known to grow in an extinct volcano crater on an island in Hawaii.

The most widely-used vegetable in the world is the onion. More than 9 billion kg (20 billion lbs) are produced each year.

Some drugs come from plants. Digitalis comes from the foxglove and is used for treating heart disease.

Stinging nettles are used in herbal medicines as cures for rheumatism.

Mint has been used as a food flavouring for a long time. It is grown commercially in the USA and used to flavour gums, toothpaste and a variety of drugs.

The Norway spruce (Christmas Tree) first grew in North America 80 million years ago.

Giant plants grow high up on Mount Kenya where the forests are covered in fog and mist. The lobelias there can reach a height of 8m (26ft).

A Rare Bloom

The giant puya plant of Mexico blooms only once in its 150 years of life – and then dies! Hundreds of little flowers appear in the last few days of its life when the plant grows to a height of 6m (20ft).

There is an evergreen tree growing in the hot climate of countries near the equator called a chocolate tree. The beans (seeds) are used for making chocolate.

If you pick an orange too early it will remain unripe. Oranges refuse to ripen unless on the tree, unlike most fruit which will ripen after picking.

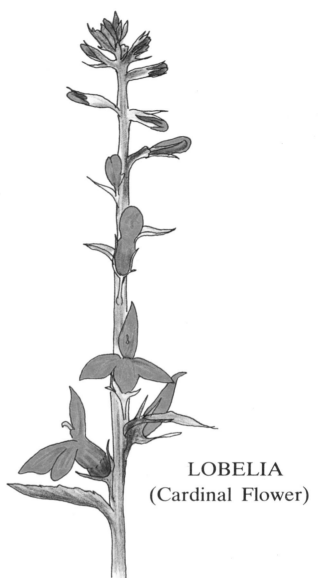

LOBELIA
(Cardinal Flower)

DAISY

During World War II oranges were so rare in England that some children ate them whole when they were first given one. They did not realise that they should have been peeled.

In Old English the daisy was called 'a daeges eage', 'the eye of the day', because it reminded people of the sun.

Pepper was such a valuable commodity in medieval Europe that there were instances of men selling their wives in exchange for it.

During the Middle Ages, when meat used in cooking was often rancid, the meats of the rich were often perfumed with musk, violets, roses, primroses and hawthorn flowers.

In Venezuela there is a tree with sap that is sweet and creamy like milk. The locals 'milk' the cowtree, as it is known, by making cuts into the bark and collecting the fluid which exudes in little cups. Scientists report it as being almost as nutritious as cows' milk.

An Apple A Day Keeps The Doctor Away

There is no evidence to substantiate this saying. Apples do not contain any magical ingredients. However, they do give us much of the potassium we need. This, combined with other minerals, helps to keep us healthy.

Did you know that there are nearly 10,000 different varieties of apple?

If you went into a restaurant a few hundred years ago, you might be a little confused on reading the menu — tea would be written as 'tay' and an apple would appear as 'a napple'.

You would not, however, find any tomatoes on the menu — they would be out in the garden as at that time they were considered poisonous and used as unusual garden plants.

You would, without doubt, find broad beans on the menu — they are the oldest vegetable known.

One of the orchid species has pods which each hold about 70 million tiny seeds.

Did you know?

There is less sugar in 1kg (2·2046lbs) of strawberries than in the same weight of lemons.

Over a third of the world's supply of pineapples is grown on the small islands of Hawaii.

Bananas grow in a bunch with their ends pointing upwards.

A poultice of boiled turnips was once used to cure chilblains.

Water lily roots mixed with tar were supposed to be a cure for baldness.

Some radishes grow so large that they can be carved into funny shapes. It is not unusual for radishes grown in Australia to weigh as much as 11kg (24lbs) each.

It used to be thought that not only would hanging mistletoe from the rafters attract kisses, but it would also protect against lightning.

A seventeenth century book seriously advised readers to plant a lily in their gardens as it was an effective method of keeping ghosts away.

In nineteenth century England some shopkeepers sold a mixture of ash and dried elder leaves as tea.

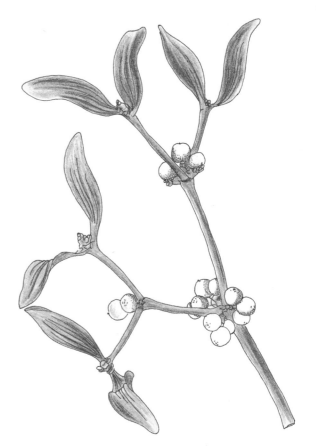

MISTLETOE

Young girls in medieval England adorned their beds with holly at Christmas time to save them from goblins.

Some people gather seaweed, boil it and eat it like cabbage or use it to make bread.

When potatoes were first introduced in France, peasants refused to grow them because they were convinced that they caused plague and leprosy.

To popularise the growing of potatoes, Louis XVI of France once wore potato flowers in his button-hole and Marie Antoinette wore garlands of them in her hair.

It was once common for sufferers from rheumatism to carry around potatoes until they were rotten in the belief that this would cure their affliction.

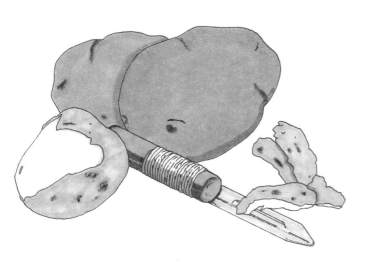

Leaves growing on a Eucalyptus tree hang vertically.

Holly leaves become less prickly the higher they grow on the tree.

On warm, windy days as much as 680 litres (150 gallons) of water may be given off by a mature beech tree.

Plants Made Coal

By the time of the Carboniferous Period (345–280 million years ago) land plants were well-established. Much of Europe, Asia and North America was covered by swamps and vast tropical forests. These swamps were eventually buried and compressed to form coalfields.

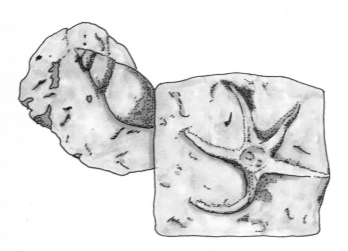

TWO FOSSILS

Many plant fossils from the Carboniferous (meaning coal bearing) Period have been found.

COAL DIAGRAM (Peat Forming Swamp) 1

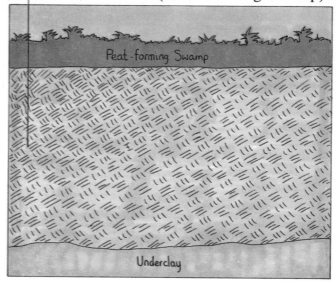

Peat-forming Swamp

Underclay

COAL DIAGRAM (Compressed Peat) 2

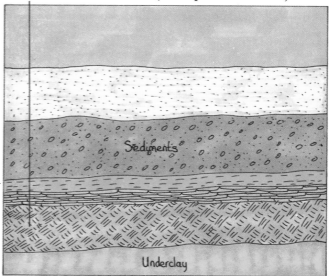

Sediments

Underclay

COAL DIAGRAM (Vegetation) 3

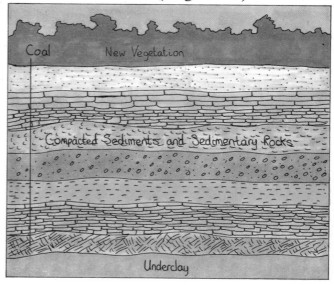

Coal   New Vegetation

Compacted Sediments and Sedimentary Rocks

Underclay

The Animal Kingdom

There are about 1,250,000 species of animals living on Earth. They are divided into the invertebrates (animals without backbones) and the vertebrates (animals with backbones).

Family Groups

Insects form the largest group with about 1,000,000 species. There are more than 20,000 fish species, 8,600 bird, 6,000 reptile and 2,500 amphibian. There are only 4,500 mammal species.

Insects

Insects were the first animals to fly. It is believed that insects evolved from a centipede-like ancestor dating from the carboniferous period 345 million years ago. The earliest known insect was a tiny springtail.

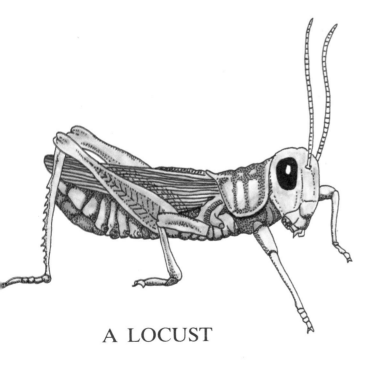

A LOCUST

Today there are at least 160,000 species of moths and butterflies, 350,000 species of beetles, about 10,000 of bees, wasps and ants, 75,000 of flies and some 50,000 bug species.

Insects develop by metamorphosis. (They change forms during their life cycle.)

The Hercules beetle of Central America can measure up to 15cm (6ins).

Cockroaches are nocturnal scavengers.

A locust swarm may consist of millions and millions of insects and can do an enormous amount of damage to crops. A swarm of one million insects could consume 20 tonnes of food a day.

There is a Brazilian butterfly that has the colour and smell of chocolate.

The Atlas moth of South East Asia has a wing span of up to 30cm (12ins).

The female mosquito is able to produce 150,000,000 offspring a year.

It is astonishing to learn that an ant can lift much more weight relatively than can a man. Average man can lift a little more than his own weight, whereas an ant can lift 50 times its own weight.

A type of wasp digs a hole in sandy ground in which it deposits its eggs. Next, it kills insects and puts them with the eggs to provide a ready supply of food when its young hatch. To protect its eggs from predators, the wasp holds a pebble in its jaws to push sand into the hole and smooth the surface over.

THREE WASPS

A BEE

Cochineal comes from beetles. People in Mexico collect the beetles. They are dried and crushed to make a fine powder which is then mixed with water to make a rich dye. To make one kilo (2.2046lb) of dye, about 150,000 beetles would be needed.

Did you know?

Scientists have discovered that bees, mosquitos, wasps and other stinging insects prefer to sting girls rather than boys. Could it be that girls are made of 'sugar and spice and all things nice'?

88

Birds

Birds are the only *vertebrate* animals capable of true flight, apart from bats, which are the only flying mammal.

The first birds are thought to have evolved from the bird-hipped dinosaurs.

Flamingoes and owls first lived on Earth about 70 million years ago.

High Flyers

Most birds do not fly above 915m (3000ft) but there are some notable exceptions. Geese flying in the Himalayas in Asia have been recorded as flying at 8840m (29,000ft). A South American condor once crashed into an aircraft at 6096m (20,000ft).

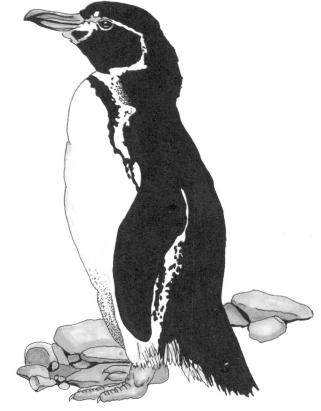

A PENGUIN

Non-Flyers

Penguins are found only south of the Equator.

OSTRICHES

The Emperor is the largest of the species. The male carries the single egg on his feet for two months to keep it from freezing. The female returns from the sea to hatch it.

The largest bird in the world is the ostrich which stands up to 2.4m (8ft) tall and may weigh 136kg (300lbs).

The ostrich is a flightless bird but a baby ostrich can run as fast as his parents – that is 64.3kph (40mph) – fast enough to escape from most hunters. And did you know that a kick from an adult ostrich is so powerful that it could break your leg?

Ostriches do NOT bury their heads in the sand.

The smallest bird is the bee humming bird which is less than 6.3cm (2½ins) long and weighs under 2.5g (0.1oz).

Fly-weight

The Helenas humming bird, found in Cuba, is so tiny that it often gets caught in spiders' webs.

Humming birds make their humming sound with their wing beats.

The trumpeter swan is one of the heaviest birds able to fly, with a weight of up to 17.2kg (38lbs).

The jacana bird, found in India, Australasia and the tropical regions of America and Africa, has long legs and extraordinarily long toes which enable it to walk on the floating leaves of water-lilies. It builds a nest which floats on the water.

The largest bird of prey is the South American condor with a wing span of about 3m (9.75ft).

Birds of prey only eat when they are hungry. After a large meal they may not kill for several days, if not weeks.

We always describe keen sight as being 'eagle-eyed' and that is a pretty good description. The eagle has probably the best vision of all birds of prey. Fish eagles can see fish swimming under water from a great height and make a power dive on to their prey.

There is one bird that can fly all day long without even flapping its wings. It is the albatross.

A wandering albatross can have a wing span of 3.5m (11.5ft) or more.

Young at Heart

Falcons are the longest-lived inhabitants of the bird world.

A FALCON'S HEAD

The 'O-O' bird is a native of Hawaii.

The aptly-named tailor bird of India and China, after selecting a suitable leaf, actually sews the edges neatly together with fibre, thus forming a pocket in which it builds its nest.

The long-legged pink flamingo gets its lovely hue from the tiny shrimp-like water creatures that it eats. Deprived of this food, the bird's plumage turns white. It's the only bird that eats its food upside down. To do this it hangs its head and swishes the top part of its beak over the water and mud, bringing its food to the surface.

Would you believe?

The owl has no movement in its eyes but to compensate for this it can revolve its head in an almost complete circle.

A FLAMINGO

A SECRETARY BIRD

Hawks have very good eyesight. Their eyes have good side vision and so the bird need not move its head when searching for food and they can pinpoint objects with great accuracy – hence the expression – 'eyes like a hawk's'.

A kiwi's beak is so sensitive that it can detect the presence of worms deep in the soil.

There is a bird called a secretary bird that lives on the grasslands of Africa. They have been seen tearing out clumps of grass, tossing them in the air with their feet and running along to catch the clumps with their beaks.

The specially bred Onagadori cocks of Japan attain tail feathers 9.1m (30ft) long. Samurai warriors used to adorn themselves in Onagadori feathers.

91

Using tools is not only a human accomplishment. Lots of creatures of all species adapt things around them for use. One bird uses a thorn to dig out grubs from rotten wood whilst the aptly-named butcher bird spikes mice and voles on a thorn bush, providing a larder for when he needs a snack. Seagulls are fond of clams but the shells are too hard for the seagull's beak so it carries the clams over rocks and drops them to crack open the shell.

Pirate of the Skies

There is one seabird that lives mainly by robbing other seabirds. It is the frigate bird which will 'buzz' other birds carrying fish in their bills, causing them to drop their catch. The robber then deftly catches its prize in mid-air.

Globe Trotter

A seabird which makes the longest nesting flight in the world actually travels from one end of the Earth to the other. It is the Arctic tern which nests in the Arctic and then journeys to winter in the Antarctic.

The dodo bird of Mauritius was extinct by the year 1681. European settlers changed the natural surroundings of the bird and took away its food supply.

A TERN AND A SEAGULL

A DODO

92

Mammals

Mammals are one of the most varied and successful groups of animals living on Earth. The brain is highly developed.

Apart from the duck-billed platypus and the anteater, all young mammals are carried inside the mother and supplied with oxygen and food until their birth. After they are born, most young mammals are fed and protected by the adults.

Unlike human beings, dogs and many other animals cool their bodies by panting. Cats sweat in an invisible way – through the pads of their feet.

The koala, a marsupial mammal found only in Australia and commonly called the native bear, is not a member of the bear family. It spends most of its life up blue-gum or eucalyptus trees feeding exclusively on their leaves from which it receives both food and moisture.

A CHEETAH

A SHIRE HORSE

Some Sprinter

The fastest creature on four legs is the cheetah, which has been known to top 112.5kph (70mph) when chasing its prey. A racehorse travels at 75.6kph (47mph).

The huge shire horses of today are descended from the warhorses of the medieval knights which were specially bred to carry the enormous weight of armour worn in those days.

Hippopotamus actually means 'river horse'. Although clumsy and ungainly on land, these animals are extremely agile in water. They can actually run along the bed of a river.

Timid Tiger

The Barbary mouse, of North Africa, has stripes similar to those of a tiger.

93

The Pygmy Mouse

This mouse, which is found in the hot areas of East Africa, is so small it could sit in a teaspoon. In order to have a drink in the morning it piles little pebbles in front of its burrow each night. The warmth of the burrow meeting the colder night air forms a dew on the pebble barricade.

Gorillas are vegetarians. Even though they look fierce they never kill in order to eat.

There are several species of kangaroo, some measuring 1.53m (5ft) in length of body with a tail over 1.23m (4ft) long. The smallest is about the size of a rabbit. The kangaroo is not constructed to run but can bound along with its powerful hind legs at speeds of up to 64.3kph (40mph) in leaps of up to 6m (19½ft).

A KANGAROO

A new-born kangaroo measures only 1.9cm (¾ins) but stays in its mother's pouch until it is fully developed.

Did you know that in Australia the sheep population, of some 148 million, is higher than that of the human population?

Trailer Tail

A certain breed of sheep in the East stores fat in its tail in much the same way that a camel does in its hump. The tail grows so big that the shepherds fit them with little carts to prevent them dragging on the ground.

Did you know that an African elephant weighs as much as 80 or 90 men?

The elephant is the only animal with four knees.

AN AFRICAN ELEPHANT

Some Swimmer

Amazing isn't it, but yes, elephants can and do swim. Their top speed is 3.2kph (2mph). They can't jump though.

The men who are the elephant keepers of India use a language to control the animals which is over 1,500 years old.

'Guinea' is a term used for a region along the coast of West Africa. The 'Guinea-pig' is a rodent native to South America but it probably got its name from the first ships that visited Guinea. A 'guinea' was the name of a gold coin used in Britain, so named because it was made from gold mined in the Guinea region.

The aardvark is probably known to many people because in a lot of dictionaries it is the first word to appear. The name comes from the Afrikaans and means 'earth-pig'.

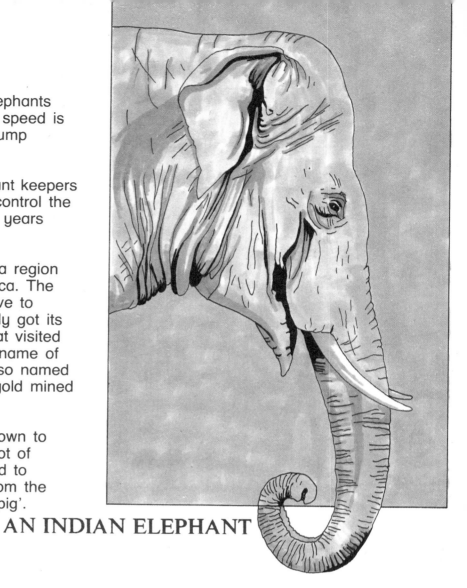

AN INDIAN ELEPHANT

The animal has long ears, sharp claws and a long, sticky tongue and, although resembling a pig in some ways, it is a relative of the anteater. It uses its sharp claws to dig out ants' nests and it can burrow faster than a man can dig with a spade. It is a nocturnal animal about 1.53m (5ft) long and lives on the ants and termites it catches with its sticky tongue. It lives in Africa.

AN AARDVARK

The flying squirrel does not really fly but glides, sometimes 30m (97.5ft) at a time. The flying squirrel has flaps of skin between the front and back legs. To move from tree to tree the animal leaps in the direction it wants to go, opens its legs, stretching the skin flap as it does so, and glides safely to its target. It is amazing the accuracy that it attains.

Another mammal that enjoys flitting from tree to tree is the chimpanzee. Although a fully-grown chimpanzee can weigh up to 76.5kg (12st), it is capable of supporting its weight on one finger when swinging from branch to branch.

Another tree dweller and expert trapeze artist is the orang-utan found in Malaya. The name means 'Old Man of the Woods'.

Bulls are not angered by the colour red. They are colour blind and are poorly sighted so when they see anything that looks like danger to them they immediately chase it.

Not only the cow and the goat are used for milk and cheese making. In some parts of the world farmers milk reindeer, llamas, camels and yaks.

A TIGER

A GIRAFFE

Did you know the giraffe is truly a 'dumb' animal, being unable to make any vocal sound? Also, in spite of its extra long neck, it has only the same number of bones in its neck as a mouse has – seven!

Forty-five to fifty years ago there were an estimated 50,000 tigers in India. Today there are about 2,000 left.

Since the 1600s at least 36 species of mammals have become extinct. Today, some 120 are in danger.

PLACES

Countries

In 1990 there were 168 independent countries in the world.

There are about three and half times as many countries north of the Equator as south of it.

The USSR is the largest country with a land area of 22,402,000sq km (8,649,412 sq miles). Canada is the second largest country.

The Vatican City, Rome, is the smallest self-governing state in the world. It is the home of the Pope and about 1000 other people including 100 Swiss Guards. It covers an area of 44 hectares (109 acres). Since 1929 it has had its own flag, postage stamps, National Anthem and radio station.

There are more than 13,000 islands forming the country of Indonesia.

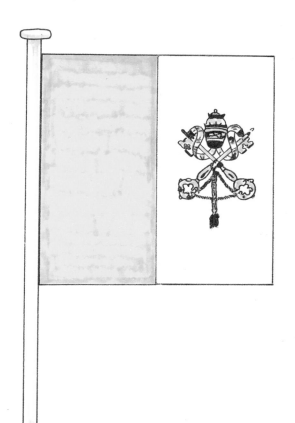

VATICAN CITY STATE FLAG

Austria, Hungary and Switzerland are some of the world's 26 countries that do not have a coastline.

The coastline of Canada is 250,000km (155,000 miles) long.

The frontier between Canada and the USA is 6,400km (3,976.9 miles) long.

The Price of Canada – One Penny

Sir William Alexander, the Earl of Stirling (1567–1640) received a grant from James I of all the lands of Canada, Nova Scotia, all the bays, rivers, islands, mines and forests. The price was one Scottish penny payable on Christmas Day.

Yet the Earl died insolvent having spent a fortune in an attempt to develop his vast estate.

America was named after Amerigo Vespucci, a merchant and explorer who sailed to the mainland several years after Columbus discovered the new world.

Lapland is the name of a region that includes parts of four countries. They are the Soviet Union, Finland, Sweden and Norway. The name is taken from the people who live there, called Lapps.

Switzerland's name is derived from the name Schwyz, a region that was important in the early history of the nation, but no one calls it by that name now. To a French-speaking resident it is La Suisse, to a German die Schweiz and to an Italian Svizzera. However, the Swiss do not use any of these names on their stamps. They use the old Latin name of Helvetia.

REINDEER

From Country to Country

The longest single road on earth is the Pan-American Highway. It begins in Alaska, passes through Canada, the USA, Mexico and all the way down the western coast of South America to Chile. It is over 27,353km (17,000 miles) long.

Brazil is the largest country in South America with almost half the continent's land area.

Africa's population is increasing by about three per cent a year, faster than that of any other continent.

The oil-producing states of Kuwait and Qatar are the world's richest countries.

Iran, or Persia as it used to be called, is the world's oldest country.

The world's largest religion is Christianity.

The second largest is Islam.

In 1945 the United Nations was founded with 51 members. There are now 157 members who meet at the UN Headquarters in New York (USA).

The countries which produce the most cotton are China, USA, USSR, India and Pakistan. Cotton was first made into clothes 30,000 years ago.

The countries which produce the most rubber are Malaysia, Indonesia, Thailand, India and Sri Lanka. Rubber comes from latex (the sap of the rubber tree).

Most of the world's tobacco is grown in China, USA, India and Brazil.

The American Indians were the first people to smoke tobacco.

UNITED NATIONS EMBLEM

AN INDIAN PIPE

The largest producers of nuclear fuel (uranium) are Canada, USA, South Africa and Australia. One tonne of uranium can produce the same amount of energy as 20,000 tonnes of coal.

South Africa produces the most gold. Gold can be beaten extremely thin. A wire about 85km (52.8 miles) can be made from 28g (1oz) of pure gold.

Cities and Towns

Jericho, in Jordan, is the oldest town in the world. People have lived there for almost 10,000 years.

The world's oldest capital city is Damascus, Syria.

Many of the towns and cities throughout Europe grew up around castles and forts.

Windsor Castle in England is the official home of the Queen of England. It is the largest inhabited castle in the world and is more than 530m (one third of a mile) long and 164m (540ft) wide, covering an area of 9 hectares (23 acres).

There are over 16 million people living in and around Mexico City. The population is rapidly increasing and may have almost doubled by the year 2000.

La Paz (Bolivia) is the highest capital city at 3,631m (11,913ft) above sea level.

Punta Arenas (Chile) is the southernmost city in the world.

Reykjavik (Iceland) is the most northerly capital city. Wellington (New Zealand) is the most southerly capital city. The distance between them is 20,000km (12,500 miles).

The city of Venice (Italy) is built on islands in a lagoon. A system of canals serves as streets and roads. People use boats to travel from place to place.

A Town

There is a town in Sweden called A.

A Bargain Buy

In 1626 a Dutchman bought Manhattan Island from some local Indians for 24 dollars-worth of trinkets. He called his town New Amsterdam. It was later re-named New York. Today Manhattan Island is probably the most expensive land anywhere in the world.

Buildings, Structures and Monuments

The Seven Wonders of the Ancient World were:–

1. The Pyramids at Giza, Egypt
2. The Hanging Gardens of Babylon, Iraq
3. The Tomb of King Mausolus, Turkey
4. The Temple of Diana, Ephesus, Turkey
5. The Colossus of Rhodes, Greece
6. The Statue of Zeus, Olympia, Greece
7. The Pharos (lighthouse) of Alexandria, Egypt.

Today, only the Pyramids are still standing. All the rest have been destroyed by earthquake, fire and invaders.

The Great Pyramid of Cheops was built between 4 and 3 thousand years BC. It took 100,000 men 20 years to construct using 2,300,000 huge stone blocks which weighed an average of 2 tonnes each. Forty men were needed to manhandle each block into place.

The Ancient Egyptians did all their measuring with knotted string, yet they were so accurate they never made more than 1.27cm ($\frac{1}{2}$ins) error. It is the tallest pyramid at 146m (480ft) high.

Where is the World's Largest Pyramid?

One normally associates pyramids with Ancient Egypt but, surprisingly, the world's largest pyramid is in Mexico. It is called the Quetzalcoatl and was built around the year 100. It is made of sun-dried bricks and earth and, although only 53.9m (177ft) high, it covers an area of 18.2 hectares (45 acres).

Stonehenge, Britain's famous stone circle, dates from about 4,800 years ago. The largest stones weigh over 50 tonnes and it took more than 1,500 years to build the monument.

STONEHENGE

The Sphinx, which stands on the banks of the Nile in Egypt, is thought to have been built with the head in the image of King Chephren and with the body of a crouching lion. It guards the tomb of King Chephren and was worshipped as a god.

The Longest Wall in the World

The Great Wall of China dates from 214 BC. It was built to protect China from invasion and is over 3000km (1864 miles) long. In places the wall is up to 10m (32ft) thick and 12m (40ft) high.

The Great Wall of China is the only man-made structure that astronauts can see from outer space through a telescope.

The Eiffel Tower, Paris, France

When Gustave Eiffel designed his famous tower, objectors said that it would be a hazard for birds. It was completed in May 1889 and was the tallest structure in the world for almost fifty years.

SPHINX

The Leaning Tower of Pisa

The Leaning Tower of Pisa took 174 years to build and it began to lean before it was finished.

In New York State (USA,) is a monument to a left leg. It was erected to symbolize a wound received by Benedict Arnold in The War of Independence. He was a hero then, but later he went over to the British side.

The Statue of Liberty

Towering above New York (USA) harbour, the Statue of Liberty has been a symbol of hope and freedom for millions of immigrants to the United States. The 93m (301ft) statue and base were a gift from the people of France, money being raised by voluntary contributions from French citizens to mark the centenary of the American revolution in 1876.

STATUE OF LIBERTY

Buddhist Beliefs

Sacred Tooth

In the temple of the Sacred Tooth in Sri Lanka (Ceylon) is a piece of bone worshipped by over 400,000,000 people who believe it to be the left eye-tooth of Buddha.

Hair Balance

The Kyaik-Hto-Yo pagoda in Burma is built on a huge boulder which stands on the very brink of a chasm.

The locals believe the rock is balanced on a hair from the head of Buddha.

The World's Tallest Buildings

The tallest is the Sears Tower in Chicago (USA). It has 110 storeys and is 443m (1453ft) high.

New York (USA) has many skyscrapers. Its tallest is the World Trade Centre at 411m (1348ft) high. The Empire State Building is 381m (1250ft) high.

The world's first skyscraper was erected in Chicago (USA) in 1884. The ten-storey building was designed by William Jenney.

Did You Know?

The world's tallest statue is on a hill near the Russian city of Volgograd? It is the figure of a lady holding a sword. The name of the statue is 'Motherland'.

The largest tomb on earth is 485.8m (1594ft) long? It measures 304.8m (1,000ft) in width and is 45.7m (150ft) high. This mound is near Osaka (Japan); Nintoku, a Japanese emperor who ruled in the fourth and early fifth century, is supposed to lie there.

The bridge over the Humber River (England) is the longest single span suspension bridge in the world. It is 1410m (4626ft) across. The Humber Bridge took 9 years to build and was opened to traffic in 1981.

HUMBER BRIDGE

During the Anglo-American War of 1812 a British force captured Washington (USA), burning many of the city's public buildings. One of the buildings set on fire was the President's mansion but not much damage was done. A coat of whitewash was sufficient to cover the smokestains and thereafter the building was to be known as the White House.

The Ashmolean Museum in Oxford (England) dates from 1679. It is the oldest museum in the world.

In London

One of the reasons why the Houses of Parliament in London (England) were built on the banks of the Thames was to prevent the buildings being surrounded by the London mob.

Marble Arch was originally built as the main entrance to Buckingham Palace. After it had been built it was discovered that it was too narrow to allow a stagecoach to pass through.

In America

The domed white Capitol is the symbol of the nation's democracy where elected Senators and Representatives meet in separate wings to make laws.

THE CAPITOL

Statue to Nothing

In Camden, Maine (USA) there stands an 8.5m (28ft) statue of one Captain Hanson Gregory. It was erected to commemorate the fact that he invented the hole in the doughnut.

THE BEGINNING OF HISTORY

History goes back 5,500 years to the first known writing. Written records provide details of events that took place in the past.

The Wheel – an important invention

About 5,000 years ago the wheel was invented. The first wheels were solid. Man's use of the wheel changed a whole way of life. Carts (the first wheeled vehicles) were made. Man used his oxen to pull them. Wider and smoother tracks were needed because the carts could not travel through forests or over rough ground. The first roads were made. Man then began to use the wheel in other ways and simple machines were invented.

War Chariot

By about 2,000 BC, wild horses had been tamed by nomads in Iran. The chariot was invented using lighter, spoked wheels that turned round the axle. More distant countries were invaded and conquered with the new war weapon and this led to the spread of new ideas from one place to another.

IRON AGE WEAPON
AND HELMET

The Alphabet

The Phoenician alphabet came into use about 1,500 BC. Phoenicians invented separate symbols for each sound so that words could be built up out of them. All the alphabets in use today have been derived from the Phoenician letters.

Exploration By Sea

By 1,100 BC the Phoenicians had begun exploring by sea. They used oars as well as sails and navigated by the stars. They reached the coasts of southern Europe and North Africa.

Iron Age

The Iron Age began about 1,000 BC. Nations with iron tools and weapons were more successful in warfare.

Books

Around 600 BC people who wanted books had to have copies made by a scribe. It took a long time so books were rare and expensive. Only the rich could own them and a library would consist of a few books.

Pompeii

In AD 79 the city of Pompeii (Italy) was buried under 6m (20ft) of lava and ash when the volcano Vesuvius erupted. Excavations have taken place and visitors to the site can now see streets and buildings preserved by the ash.

Ancient Civilisations

Egypt

Five thousand years ago Egyptian civilisation began. The territories along the River Nile shared the same language and culture and they united to form the first nation. Egyptian religion was concerned with life after death and dead bodies were preserved as mummies.

KING TUTANKHAMUN

The kings of Egypt were called pharaohs and worshipped as sun gods and called 'a son of the sun god'. The Egyptians believed that their sun god rode across the sky each day. A pharoah would have a tomb for when he died built in the shape of a pyramid. Every pyramid had four sides, one of which faced east. It was believed that when a pharaoh died he would wait for his father's approach as the sun rose from the east and at midday, when the sun fell on all four slopes of the pyramid, a staircase was formed for the pharaoh's soul to climb.

The treasures of Tutankhamun were found in 1922 by Howard Carter, an Englishman who had been searching for the boy-king's tomb for twenty years. Inside the tomb were four rooms filled with more than 500 objects.

The oldest glass objects known were found in tombs dating from 2,500 BC.

The oldest board game originated in ancient Egypt. Cone-shaped pieces were raced to the finish – not unlike the popular game of Monopoly.

China

Agriculture developed in the valley of the Yellow River. This resulted in the civilisation of China. China's written history dates back about 3,500 years. By 1,500 BC the Chinese were making silk from the cocoons of certain caterpillars. They also invented the compass, gunpowder, porcelain, paper and an early computer called an abacus. This was a simple calculator using beads which were moved along wires. The abacus is still in use today, as is the wheelbarrow which was invented in China about 1,600 years ago.

A SILK WORM

Greece

Greek civilisation began about 4,000 years ago. Because Greece is a mountainous country the Greeks established small city states. The state of Athens was the first place in the world to establish democratic government.

THE ACROPOLIS

Ancient Greek philosophers (thinkers) are renowned for their contribution to our knowledge of the world.

In Ancient Greece:–

A Spartan man who had not married by the age of thirty lost his right to vote.

Boxing matches began with the two opponents standing face to face, their noses touching.

Playing with the yo-yo was one of the favourite pastimes.

Fashionable women dyed their parasols in the colours of their favourite chariot teams.

The Ancient Greeks believed it was unmanly to have a *hot* bath.

According to legend the city of Rome was founded in 753 BC. At its height, about 105 AD, the Roman Empire stretched across much of North Africa and the Middle East and more than half of Europe.

The Romans were clever builders and engineers. They laid water pipes and drains, built public baths (with central heating) and great outdoor theatres like the Colosseum in Rome. They built cities and a road system that has lasted for 2,000 years.

In Ancient Rome all those wishing to be elected to official positions wore white togas before the elections were held. The word 'candidate' comes from the Latin word 'candidus' meaning white.

A ROMAN SOLDIER

ROMAN TOGA

Part of a Roman soldier's pay was made in salt, known as 'Salarium'. That is why pay of today is known as a salary.

The Ancient Romans first played a game like golf using bent wooden sticks and a leather ball stuffed with feathers.

The early Romans probably used cattle as a form of currency.

The Roman Emperor, Caligula, housed his favourite horse in a marble stall and had it fed from a golden manger. He even made it a consul.

The Crossbow

The first mechanised hand weapon was the crossbow, invented about 1050 AD in France. The bolt could travel 305m (1000ft) or more.

The Battle of Hastings

William, Duke of Normandy (France), defeated King Harold in 1066. He became King William I of England. The battle was not at Hastings but at Senlac Hill about 9.6km (6 miles) away.

The Crusades

Large armies of Christian knights and noblemen travelled across Europe to the Holy Land (Palestine) to free the country from the Turks and to recapture the temple at Jerusalem for the Christians. They did not succeed.

Henry II

He introduced the yard as a unit of measurement. It was to be the distance between his nose and his outstretched thumb.

A CRUSADER

The Longest War

Edward III of England wanted to be king of France. He began the Hundred Years' War in 1338 and war against France lasted until 1453.

Philip VI of France was not one of the best generals in history. It is recorded that at the Battle of Crecy in 1346 his army lost over 4,000 men but only managed to kill 100 of their English adversaries.

The Black Death

In 1333 the bubonic plague started in the Far East. It was spread by fleas which bit rats. It is estimated that the plague killed a third of the world's population.

109

Henry V

In 1415 Henry V of England led his armies to victory at the Battle of Agincourt. The English longbow archers defeated a much larger French force.

Germ Warfare in the Middle Ages

Soldiers besieging towns and castles in the Middle Ages used to catapult decaying carcasses of animals over the defensive walls to spread disease.

Henry VI

Henry VI succeeded to the thrones of England and France at the age of nine months on August 31st 1422.

Jeanne d'Arc – Joan of Arc

In 1429 a peasant girl, Jeanne d'Arc, placed herself at the head of the French armies. She claimed that she was sent by God. She led the French to many victories but was convicted of witchcraft and burnt to death in Rouen in 1431.

James IV

In 1457 James IV banned a golf-like game in Scotland because he feared his soldiers would not devote enough time to practise their archery skills.

Christopher Columbus

Christopher Columbus set sail from Portugal in 1492 to try to find a new route to India. Instead, he discovered North America. Columbus thought he had reached India and so he called the people he had found Indians.

Portuguese Navigation

In 1519 Ferdinand Magellan, a Portuguese navigator, led the first voyage around the world. Magellan named a new ocean the Pacific. He was killed in the Philippines. Only one of his five ships reached home safely in 1522. The expedition around the world had taken three years.

columbus   magellan

Henry VIII

This English king married six times. He had two daughters and one son.

Edward VI, son of Henry VIII and Jane Seymour, succeeded his father to the throne in 1547 at the age of nine. He died of consumption in 1553. His reign had lasted only six years.

Duel Deaths

In the eight years between 1601 and 1609 two thousand noble Frenchmen died in duels.

The Great Fire of London 1666

Although the fire destroyed over 13,000 houses and 89 churches, as well as hospitals and warehouses, etc, only six people lost their lives. One good thing about the fire was that it helped to check the plague which was rife in London at the time.

King George II

When King George II's horse bolted during the early stages of the Battle of Deltingen, Bavaria, in 1743, the King took his place at the head of his troops on foot, the last British king to do so.

HENRY VIII

Captain Cook

Did you know that in the eighteenth century Captain James Cook discovered a group of 150 islands? These tropical islands in the South Pacific became known as the nation of Tonga. They lie astride an imaginary line where one day ends and another begins. Because each calendar day begins at the International Date Line, Tonga is said to be called 'the place where time begins'.

The Lutine Bell

The famous Lutine Bell which hangs in the hall of the large Lloyd's insurance house in London was originally from the sailing frigate 'La Lutine'. She sank in 1799 during a storm off the Dutch coast. The bell is still rung to indicate important announcements. One ring indicates bad news and two rings indicates good news.

LUTINE BELL

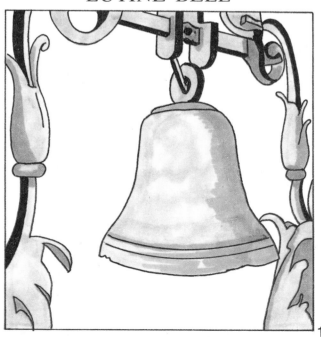

July 4th Celebrations

The Declaration of Independence was signed on July 4th 1776. This is recognised as the beginning of the United States of America.

The French Revolution

This began with the Storming of the Bastille in 1789, led to the execution of the king, Louis XVI, in 1793 and the eventual rise to power of Napoleon Bonaparte which changed the political face of Europe.

The Great Exhibition

In 1851 the Great Exhibition opened in London, England. It showed the ways in which the Industrial Revolution had changed the world.

In 1887 the Yellow River, China, flooded its banks and 9 million people died, making it the worst flood disaster ever.

NAPOLEON

ADOLF HITLER

World War I

The First World War lasted from 4th August 1914 to November 11th 1918. During that period almost 10 million people were killed and 20 million wounded.

World War II

The Second World War began on 3rd September 1939 and finally ended in September 1945 with the surrender of the Japanese. Around 55 million people were killed.

Mount Everest is Conquered

In 1953 Edmund Hillary and Sherpa Tensing climbed to the summit of Mount Everest.

The First Man on The Moon

On July 20th 1969, Neil Armstrong (USA) became the first human being to set foot on the Moon. He said, 'That's one small step for a man; one giant leap for mankind.'

TRANSPORT

About Travel

More than 500 million passengers per year fly on the world's scheduled airline services. The largest airport in the world is Riyadh (Saudi Arabia); the busiest is Chicago's O'Hare Airport (USA) where an aircraft lands or takes off every 35 to 40 seconds.

The shortest scheduled flight lasts two minutes, flying from Westray Island to Papa Westray off Scotland (UK).

BI PLANE

Concorde travels faster than the speed of sound. It takes three hours to fly from London to New York, a distance of 5,631km (3,500 miles). Concorde has a cruising speed of 2,413.5kph (1,500mph). It came into service in 1976.

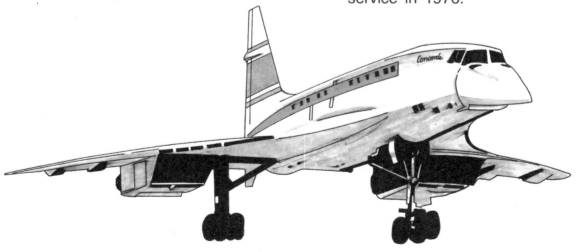

CONCORDE

The USA has more kilometres of road than any other country. It also has the most motor vehicles with one for every 1.5 people. In Chad there are 1.5 cars for every 1,000 people.

About 7½ million cars are made in the USA each year.

The Japanese are the second largest car producers with about 7 million vehicles being made each year.

The Orient Express is said to be the most luxurious form of travel. The train used to run from Paris (France) to Istanbul (Turkey). It now runs between London (England) and Venice (Italy).

Every day, about 18 million people in Japan travel on trains.

THE ORIENT EXPRESS

Train Robbers

Over £2½ million was stolen from a train in Buckinghamshire (England) in 1963. Only about one seventh of the money has since been recovered.

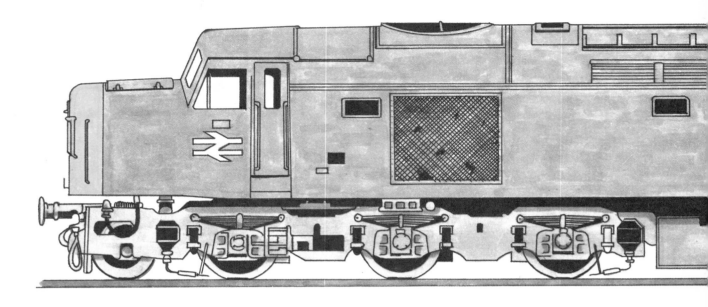

Record speeds

The British LNER locomotive 'Mallard' achieved a speed of 202.77kph (126mph) in 1938. It is the fastest ever reached by a steam train.

Two electric locomotives from France hold the world speed record for trains. In 1955 they pulled carriages at a speed of 330.8kph (205.5mph).

The fastest speed by helicopter is 368kph (228.6mph) achieved in 1978.

In 1978 the official highest speed on water, 511kph (317.5mph), was reached by K P Wardby of Australia.

The record for an Atlantic crossing on water is 62 hours 7.47 minutes achieved by the speedboat 'Gentry Eagle' in 1989.

On the Roads

The earliest vehicles were probably wooden sledges. Early Man then began to use crude log rollers to move heavy objects. The rollers needed to be picked up from the back and put down in front again to keep the load moving. These crude log rollers were the forerunners of wheels.

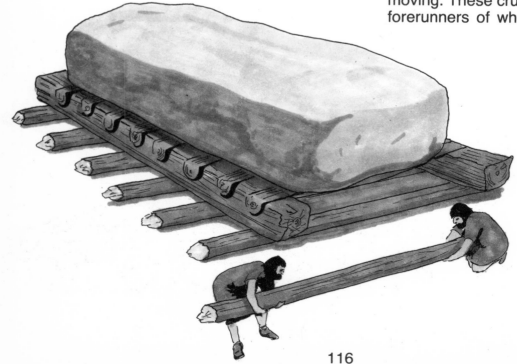

The Romans built more than 80,000km (50,000 miles) of paved roads in order to move their armies quickly to all parts of their Empire. At that time the journey from London to Rome by horse took six days — it took just as long almost 1,600 years later.

MAIN ROADS IN BRITAIN

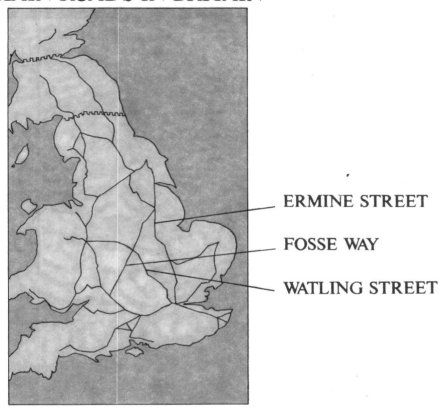

ERMINE STREET

FOSSE WAY

WATLING STREET

Stagecoaches were so called because they had to stop and change horses at various stages when travelling on long-distance routes. They came into use in the early 1600s and were still being used more than two centuries later.

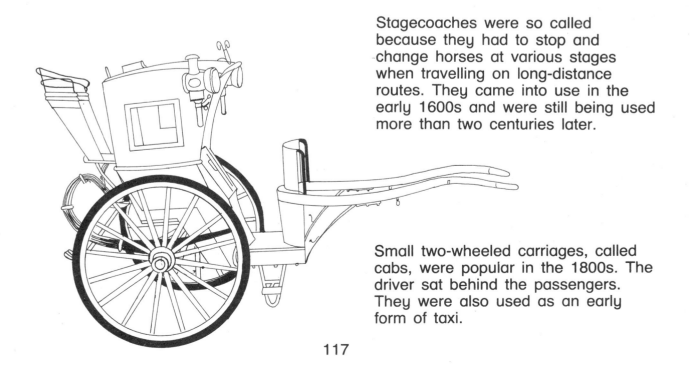

Small two-wheeled carriages, called cabs, were popular in the 1800s. The driver sat behind the passengers. They were also used as an early form of taxi.

117

The hobbyhorse was an early type of bicycle dating from the mid-17th century. It had no pedals and the rider had to push it along with his feet on the ground.

The penny-farthing bicycle was popular in the 1870s. It had pedals on a huge wheel in front and the wheel at the back was very small.

China produces about 17 million bicycles each year.

A PENNY FARTHING

In 1885 Gottlieb Daimler built the first petrol-driven motor cycle. Its fastest speed was under 19kph (11.8mph). In 1978 the motor cycle speed record was 512.73kph (318.6mph).

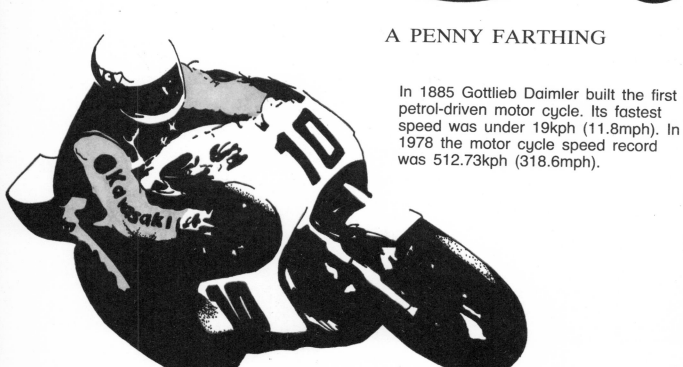

The first petrol-driven car was built in 1885 by the German engineer Karl Friedrich Benz. It had three wheels, a small one in front and two larger ones at the back. Its top speed was 14.4kph (9mph).

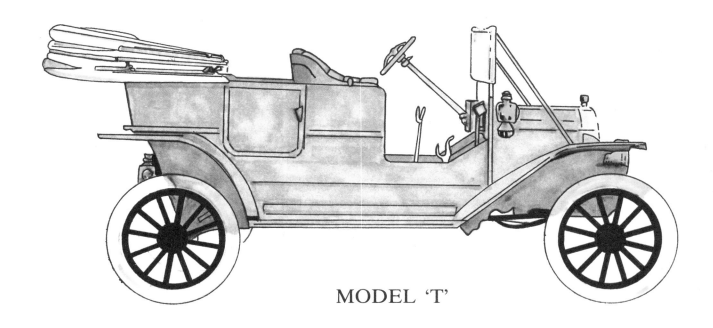

MODEL 'T'

In 1908 the mass production of cars began with the introduction of the assembly line (moving belt) by the American industrialist, Henry Ford. His Model T was the first car to be manufactured in this way.

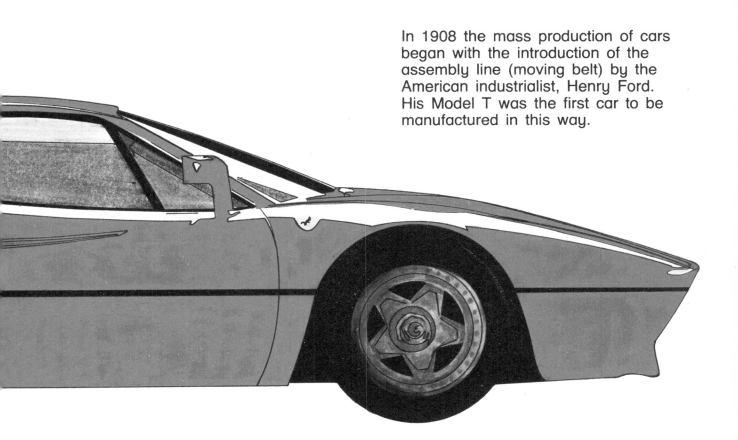

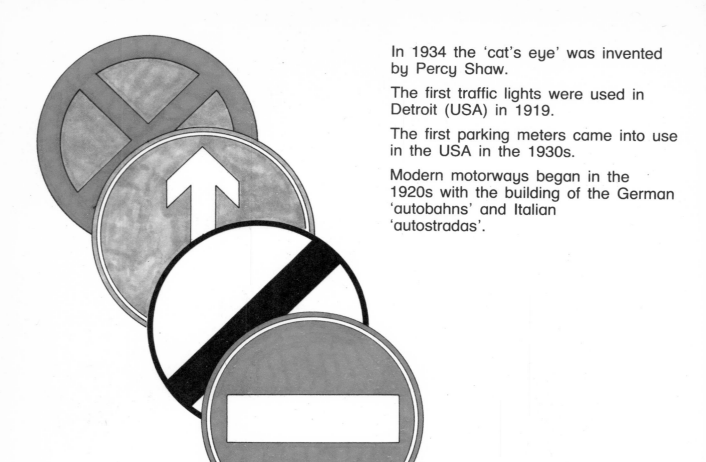

In 1934 the 'cat's eye' was invented by Percy Shaw.

The first traffic lights were used in Detroit (USA) in 1919.

The first parking meters came into use in the USA in the 1930s.

Modern motorways began in the 1920s with the building of the German 'autobahns' and Italian 'autostradas'.

Fun Facts

a) In Japan, the members of the Imperial family are the only people allowed to drive a maroon-coloured car.

b) In 1901, George Thornton, from Wales (UK), was fined for speeding. He had driven his car at 16kph (9.9mph)!

c) The first person to be imprisoned for a traffic offence was the French inventor Nicolas Cugnot. He drove his steam-powered vehicle into a wall at its top speed of about 6.4kph (4mph).

d) Because of the noise made by their diesel engines, local buses on the Caribbean island of Haiti are called 'Tap-Taps'.

And Did You Know?

e) Petrol is produced in more than thirty states in the USA.

f) There are more than 30 countries which export only one thing: oil.

At Sea

By about 6000 BC the first boats were probably being used. They were rafts made from logs lashed together and paddled by hand.

Around 5,500 years ago the Egyptians used bundles of reeds from the banks of the River Nile to build reed boats.

In the 9th and 10th centuries the Vikings explored the seas in their longships, invading and raiding all along the coasts of Europe.

A VIKING

16th Century Treasure

There are thought to be at least 2,000 Spanish galleons lying in the waters off the coasts of Florida and the Bahamas. Most of them were sunk with large amounts of gold on board.

The 'Mary Rose', built for King Henry VIII in 1510, sank off the southern coast of England in 1545. She and her contents were raised from the sea-bed in 1982.

The 'Queen Elizabeth' was the largest passenger liner at 314m (1030ft) in length and weighing more than 85,000 tonnes.

The first hovercraft, SR-N1, was launched in 1959. It was designed by the Englishman, Christopher Cockerell, who was knighted ten years later for his invention.

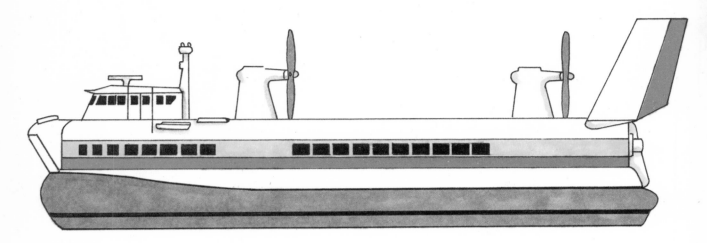

The Soviet Navy has the largest submarines in the world. They are about 170m (557.7ft) long and weigh 25,000 tonnes.

The Japanese supertanker 'Seawise Giant', built in 1976, was the largest ship ever. It was 458m (1503ft) long and could carry 565,000 tonnes of crude oil.

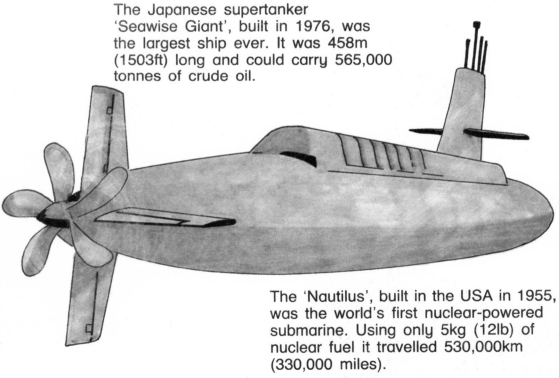

The 'Nautilus', built in the USA in 1955, was the world's first nuclear-powered submarine. Using only 5kg (12lb) of nuclear fuel it travelled 530,000km (330,000 miles).

The 'Statfiord B' is the world's largest oil platform. It was built at Stavanger in Norway. Eight tugs were needed to tow it into position. At 816,000 tonnes, it is the heaviest object ever to have been moved in one piece.

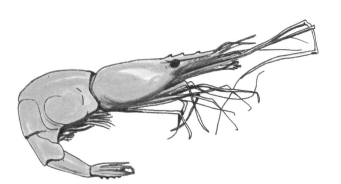

Fishy Facts

A pre-historic fish, the coelacanth, was caught in the sea off South Africa in 1938. Since then many have been caught. The fish was thought to have been extinct for 70 million years.

Almost one quarter of all the fish caught is used in the manufacture of pet food, fertilizers, glue, soap and margarine. The rest is eaten as food.

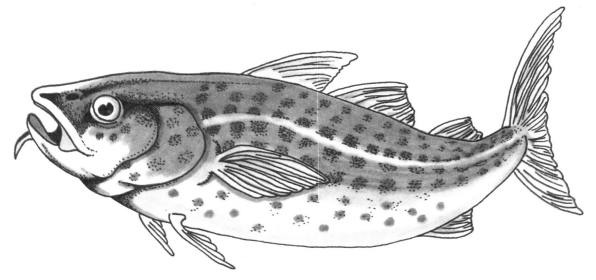

A COELACANTH

By Rail

The first steam engine was built in 1803 by the English inventor, Richard Trevithick.

In 1825 the first public railway, the Stockton and Darlington Railway, was opened using a steam engine designed by the English inventor, George Stephenson.

Queen Victoria (1837–1901) did not allow the Royal Train to travel faster than 48kph (30mph).

The fastest train is the TGV (Train à Grande Vitesse), a passenger train which runs between Lyons and Paris in France, a distance of 425km (264 miles). It can reach a speed of 270kph (168mph) but its average speed is 212.5kph (132mph). It takes two hours to complete the journey.

The Japanese 'Bullet' trains average more than 200kph (124mph).

The USA has the most kilometres of railway track.

The first underground railway opened in London (England) in 1863. It is the longest in the world with more than 400km (248 miles) of track.

When it is finished, the Channel Tunnel rail link between England and France will be 50km (31 miles) long.

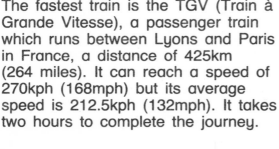
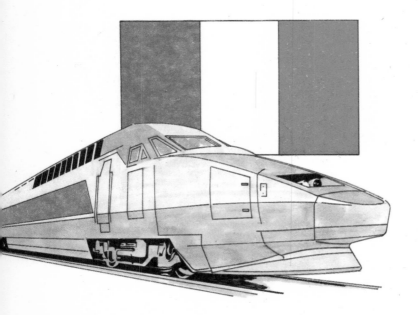

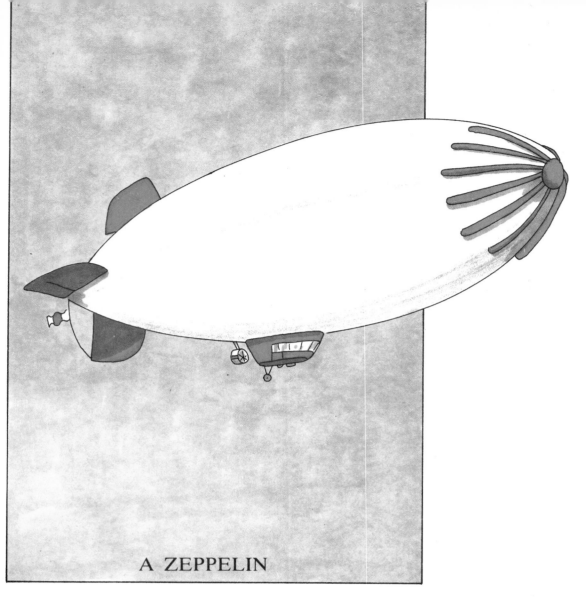

A ZEPPELIN

In The Air

When the Montgolfier brothers' hot air balloon landed after its first flight in 1783, it was hacked to pieces by villagers who thought that it was a monster from space.

Streamlined balloons were invented in 1900. They were named Zeppelins after their German inventor. A Zeppelin had an engine and a propeller which meant that the aircraft could be directed.

Travel by airship ended in the late 1930s because so many of the hydrogen-filled airships caught fire.

In 1853 the English engineer, George Cayley, built the first glider. It flew 457m (1500ft). Modern gliders are able to fly up to a height of 15,000m (49,215ft) and can travel a distance of up to 1500km (932 miles).

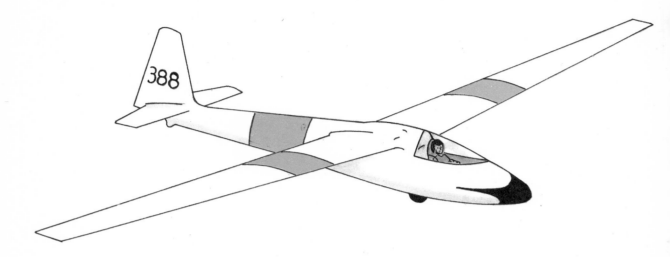

The first aeroplanes were made of canvas and wood with just a few iron parts so that they could be kept as light as possible.

The first man to fly an aeroplane was Orville Wright in 1903. The flight at Kitty Hawk, North Carolina, USA, lasted less than a minute and covered a distance of 37m (121.3ft).

The first non-stop flight across the Atlantic was made by Alcock and Brown in 1919. They flew in a Vimy bomber.

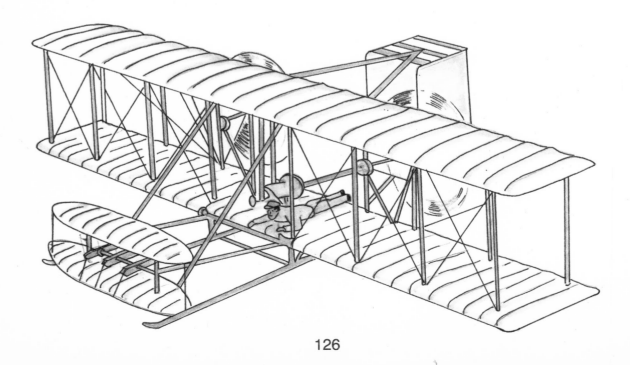

The first solo flight across the Atlantic was made in 1927 by Charles Lindbergh (USA) in 'Spirit of St Louis'. It took 33½ hours to fly from New York (USA) to Paris (France).

The first non-stop flight around the world was made by Dick Rutan and Jeana Yeagar in 'Voyager'. The year was 1986.

Giant Jumbo

The Boeing 747, the Jumbo Jet, can carry 500 passengers. It has a wing span of more than 70m (232ft) and weighs over 370 tonnes.

FAMOUS PEOPLE

Confucius

There are 40,000 direct descendants of Confucius (551–478 BC), the famous Chinese philosopher, living in China at the present time.

Socrates was a Greek philosopher who lived from about 470 to 399 BC. He is thought by many to have been the most eminent thinker in history.

Plato was a Greek philosopher who lived from about 427 to 347 BC. He was a pupil of Socrates. He founded a school for advanced studies in Athens which could be regarded as the world's first university.

Aristotle (384–322 BC) was a Greek philosopher. He was a pupil of Plato. He developed the study of logic and put forward the theory that the world was made up of four elements – earth, water, air and fire.

CONFUCIUS (551–478 BC)

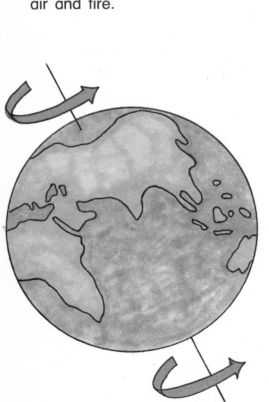

THE EARTH'S AXIS

Pythagoras lived in the 6th century BC. He was a Greek mathematician and was the first to suggest that the Earth was not flat but a sphere rotating on its axis.

Euclid was a Greek mathematician who lived about 2,300 years ago. He compiled a book called 'Elements' which contained all the geometric knowledge of his time. It was the most successful book ever written and is still studied to this day.

Aristarchos of Samos was a Greek astronomer who lived from about 310 to 250 BC. He was the first to suggest that the Earth moved round the Sun.

Ptolemy was a Greek astronomer who lived in the 2nd century AD. He claimed that the Earth lay stationary at the centre of the universe and that the Sun, the Moon and the known planets all revolved round it. His idea was believed for the next 1,400 years.

Johannes Kepler was a German astronomer who lived from 1577 to 1630. He worked out the correct movement of the planets.

Edmund Halley (1656–1742) lived in England and was the first scientist to realise that the big ball of fire seen from Earth in 1682 was on a path that would bring it back every 76 years.

EDMUND HALLEY
(1656–1742)

Sir Isaac Newton (1642–1727), the English physicist and mathematician, discovered that white light is a mixture of colours.

After watching an apple fall from a tree he worked out his Law of Universal Gravity.

He is known to have written about 100,000 pages of notes on astronomy and chemistry and although he was an excellent mathematician he was incapable of performing simple mental arithmetic.

SIR ISAAC NEWTON (1642–1727)

Charles Darwin (1809–82) was a British biologist. He sailed round the world gathering evidence from his study of rocks, plants and animals. He published a book 'On The Origin of Species' in 1859 which explains his theory of evolution.

CHARLES DARWIN
(1809–1882)

Albert Einstein (1879–1955) was a German-born physicist. He published his General Theory of Relativity, which explains gravitation, in 1916.

He was awarded the Nobel Prize for Physics in 1921.

When he was ten years old he was told by one of his schoolmasters, ''You will never amount to very much.'' ...

and ...

... he failed at his first attempt to pass the entrance examination for the Polytechnic in Zürich.

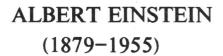

ALBERT EINSTEIN
(1879–1955)

Louis Pasteur (1822–95) the great French medical researcher, had such an obsessive fear of dirt and infection that he refused to shake hands with anyone.

He realised that bacteria made food go bad. In 1856 he discovered that a process of gentle heating (pasteurisation) killed harmful bacteria. The milk we buy today has been pasteurised.

Florence Nightingale (1820–1910), also known as The Lady With The Lamp, nursed injured soldiers in the Crimean War (1854–56). Her work laid the foundations of today's nursing profession.

Every bullring in Spain has a monument to the Scottish bacteriologist Sir Alexander Fleming (1881–1955) whose discovery of penicillin in 1928 has saved countless toreadors from dying of gangrene after being gored by bulls.

FLORENCE NIGHTINGALE
(1820–1910)

Benjamin Franklin (1706–90) was an American statesman, writer and scientist. He proved that electricity was present in lightning – he flew a kite in a thunderstorm – and invented the lightning rod.

Michael Faraday (1791–1867) was an English physicist who discovered how to generate electricity.

The American inventor Thomas Edison (1847–1931) was once expelled from a school in Ohio for being too stupid to be worth teaching.

He invented the phonograph (an early type of record player) in 1878. In 1879 he conducted more than 1,200 unsuccessful experiments before he finally succeeded in producing the first modern electric light bulb.

THOMAS EDISON (1847–1931)

Marie Curie (1867–1934) was a Polish-born scientist, working in France with her husband Pierre, who discovered radium and polonium. She pioneered the medical use of radio-activity and won two Nobel prizes – Physics (1903) and Chemistry (1911).

MARIE CURIE (1867–1934)

Marco Polo was the son of an Italian trader and went with his father and uncle to China in 1275. They stayed many years with Kublai Khan, the Chinese ruler. He sent them to explore other parts of the East. Marco Polo wrote a book about the new lands he had seen and this book was the basis of one of the first accurate maps of Asia.

MARCO POLO (1254−1324)

James Cook (1728–79) was an English explorer and navigator. He commanded the 'Endeavour' and was the first European to cross the Antarctic circle. He explored the coasts of New Zealand and eastern Australia, landing at Botany Bay in 1770. He charted the Great Barrier Reef. He was killed by natives on Hawaii.

JAMES COOK (1728−1779)

David Livingstone was a Scottish explorer who travelled to Africa in search of the source of the River Nile. He discovered Victoria Falls. In 1869 he was thought to be lost and H. M. Stanley set out to find him. Two years later Stanley found Livingstone near Lake Tanganyika.

STANLEY (1841–1904)

ROALD AMUNDSEN (1872–1928)

The Norwegian, Roald Amundsen, was the first man to reach the South Pole in 1911. This was just a few weeks ahead of the British expedition led by R. F. Scott who, with his companions, died on the return journey.

Vivien Fuchs, leading the British Commonwealth Expedition, was the first to cross Antarctica in 1957/58.

Alexander the Great (356–323 BC) was King of Macedon (Greece). He was one of the world's most capable generals. He conquered the Persian Empire and in ten years of fighting never lost a battle.

He is said to have ordered his armourers to make helmets much larger than those worn by his troops. These were left for the enemy to find in the hope that they would be afraid to fight the 'giant' soldiers.

A COIN SHOWING ALEXANDER THE GREAT

JULIUS CAESAR (about 101–44)

Julius Caesar (about 101–44 BC) was a Roman soldier and statesman who conquered much of Europe to make Rome the capital of a vast Empire.

To celebrate his victory over Pompey, he gave a banquet at which 150,000 guests were seated at 22,000 tables. It lasted for two days. He also proclaimed a rent-free year for every poor family in the Empire.

He was killed by former supporters led by Brutus.

A Battling Caesar (161–192)

Commodus Lucius Aelius Aurelius, Emperor of Rome, fought and won 1,301 battles in the gladiatorial arena. A wrestler, Narcissus, finally strangled him to death.

The Roman Emperor, Nero, would have his favourite horses dressed in human costume and when they were old he awarded them pensions.

He is also the only competitor to be awarded first place in an Olympic competition without winning or even finishing the course.

135

Attila the Hun, who died in 453 AD, the leader of the barbarian hordes that overran the Western civilisation of the age, and who was known as 'The Scourge of God', was a dwarf.

Napoleon Bonaparte (1769–1821) was Emperor of France. He was a great military leader who conquered Holland, Spain, Italy and much of Europe. He was defeated at the Battle of Waterloo in 1815.

Winston Churchill (1874–1965) was the Prime Minister of Great Britain during World War II. His leadership inspired the Allies to victory in 1945.

WINSTON CHURCHILL (1874–1965)

nelson

When Admiral Nelson lay dying at Trafalgar in 1805 he requested that his body should not be buried at sea. Unfortunately, as burial at sea was the normal naval custom, there were no facilities for embalming on board the ship. The problem was solved by having his body immersed in a large cask of brandy. When his ship, 'Victory', finally landed at Greenwich, Nelson's body was found to be in an excellent state of preservation and was eventually buried in St Paul's Cathedral.

William the Conqueror killed two men after he died.

He met his death at Rouen in 1087 when he was out riding. His horse reared and his saddle pommel was forced into his stomach causing fatal internal injuries. His body was laid out and embalmers sent for. The two unfortunates who came to do the job caught a fever from the corpse and both died within a few days.

King in Pawn

When King Richard II got married in 1380 he had to pawn the Crown Jewels to pay for the wedding.

In 1428, the 4th Earl of Salisbury became the first Englishman to use cannons in battle. He later became the first Englishman to be killed by a cannon.

THE GREAT SEAL OF WILLIAM THE CONQUEROR

A PENNY OF RICHARD II

Royal Forger

Henry VIII (1509–1547), always on the lookout for ways of swelling the royal coffers, issued 'silver' testoons which in fact were copper coins with a thin coating of silver. As the silver covering wore off the King's copper nose showed through earning him the nickname of 'Old King Coppernob'.

King August of Saxony and Poland (1670–1733) was known as 'August The Strong' and used his ten stone valet as a weight in his daily exercises on his palace balcony. He would lift the man over the parapet and stretch and bend his arms back and forth – suspending his 'weight' over a 228.6 m (750 ft) drop!

King George I of England (reigned 1714–27), ruler of Hanover from 1698, never learned to speak the language of his new subjects – English.

King William IV (1830–37) of England was also William I of Hanover, William II of Ireland and William III of Scotland.

George Washington (1732–99) first President of the USA was also its first millionaire. He died in the last hour of the last day of the week, in the last month of the last year of the century.

GEORGE WASHINGTON

(1732–1799)

Teddy bears were named after a president of the United States, Theodore (Teddy) Roosevelt.

THEODORE ROOSEVELT (1858–1919)

The Kennedy-Lincoln Coincidence

Kennedy was elected in 1960.

Lincoln was elected in 1860.

Kennedy's secretary was named Lincoln.

Lincoln's secretary was named Kennedy.

Both secretaries advised their presidents not to go to the places where they were assassinated.

Both men were shot in the presence of their wives.

**ABRAHAM LINCOLN AND
JOHN F KENNEDY**

LYNDON B JOHNSON

The successor of each president was named Johnson.

Andrew Johnson, born 1808.

Lyndon Johnson, born 1909.

Of the two assassins,

Booth was born in 1839,

Oswald was born in 1939.

Both men were killed before they could be tried.

Both presidents were deeply concerned with the Civil Rights problem of their particular time.

Lincoln and Kennedy were carried to their graves on the same caisson.

The famous German composer Johannes Brahms once earned his living by playing the piano at inns.

Probably the most prolific composer of all time was Mozart (1756–91). He died at the early age of 35, yet produced over 600 works.

In the work 'Alleluia' the title is sung over and over again – there are no other words.

After squandering a fortune on gambling Mozart sent begging letters to wealthy acquaintances.

13 – Lucky For Him

Richard Wagner, famous German composer, considered 13 to be his lucky number. He was born in 1813, had 13 letters in his name, left school at 13, wrote 13 operas, and loved 13 women in his life. His year of birth adds up to 13 and he died on February 13th 1883.

wagner

verdi

Paderewski, the famous Polish pianist and national leader, once had each finger separately insured.

A press reporter once asked the great Italian composer, Guiseppe Verdi, for his full address. "I think," replied Verdi, who was not noted for his modesty, "that Italy will be sufficient."

By the age of five the famous conductor, Leopold Stokowski, could play the violin and piano. He first conducted an orchestra when he was only twelve years old.

Molière, the great French playwright, died while playing the part of the hypochondriac in his own play 'The Imaginary Invalid'.

Mark Twain wrote most of his books in bed.

Emile Zola, the great French writer, came bottom in French Literature at school.

Leonardo da Vinci needed to see a look of real fear – so he pretended to set himself on fire to scare his housekeeper – and painted the expression of horror on her face.

Giovanni Bellini, 15th century Italian artist, was painting the scene of Salome carrying the head of John the Baptist but could not quite get the right effect. The Sultan of Turkey, who had commissioned the picture, had a slave beheaded in front of the artist. The horrified Bellini fled back to Venice.

MARK TWAIN (1835–1910)

Artist Anthony Van Dyck (1599–1641) painted King Charles the First's portrait no fewer than 36 times.

A Nose For Trouble

Cyrano de Bergerac, 17th century poet, wit and expert swordsman, fought and won 1,000 duels over insults about his over-size nose.

During one three-month period he 'ran through' four people each week.

A hand of cards containing two aces and two eights is known as Dead Man's Hand because Wild Bill Hickcock had these cards in his hand when he was shot dead during a card game in a saloon.

Henry Ford, the motor millionaire, never threw away a letter or a bill and his lawyers were left to sort out 5,000,000 documents – a two-year task.

Amongst them were 10,000 unopened letters.

Al Capone (1899–1947), the Italian-born American gangster, was leader of a crime syndicate in Chicago in the 1920s during the prohibition era.

Al Capone

Becher's Brook, one of the jumps at Aintree racecourse in England, is named after Captain Becher who fell from his horse into the brook twice in one race in 1839.

Jacques-Yves Cousteau (1910–) the French under-water explorer invented the aqua-lung and helped develop under-water filming.

Charlie Chaplin (1899–1977) was born in London, England and famed for his silent film comedies and 'Tramp' character.

The late John Wayne, the American film star, famed for his 'tough' cowboy roles, was christened Marion Morrison.

CHARLIE CHAPLIN
(1899–1977)

SCIENCE

About 450 BC the Greek philosopher Democritus was the first to suggest that all things are made of atoms. The Ancient Greeks believed that nothing could be smaller than an atom but it is now known that each atom is made of minute particles spinning around a centre or nucleus.

An important advance in science was the classification of all living things, completed by Aristotle around 350 BC.

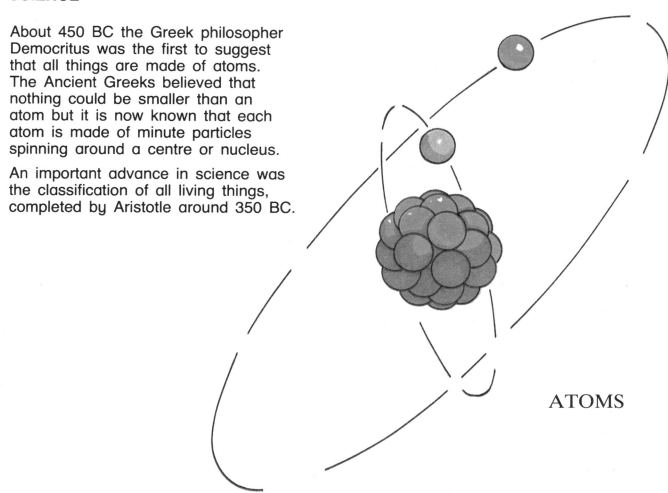

ATOMS

1–2–3–4–5–6–7–8–9 and 0

The Invention of Zero

Almost 1500 years ago some Indian mathematicians suggested the use of the symbol '0' meaning zero or nothing. By about 810 AD the Arabs had established the modern system of numerals which we use today. The plus '+' and minus '−' signs were first used in arithmetic about 1490 and the equals '=' sign by about 1557.

ARABIC NUMERALS

In 1642 a Frenchman, Blaise Pascal, built an adding and subtracting machine which was operated by gears and wheels.

The first electronic digital computer, called ENIAC (electronic numerical integrator and computer), was made in 1946 but it could not store data or programs. It was designed by the American engineers John William Mauchly and John Presper Eckart.

The first computer capable of storing and processing information was the Manchester Mark I, first used in England in 1948.

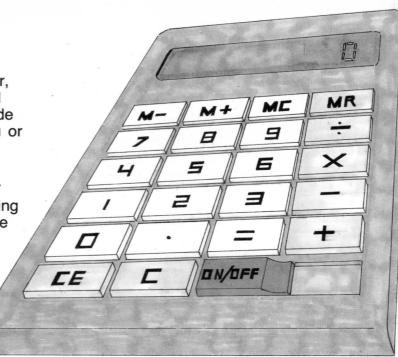

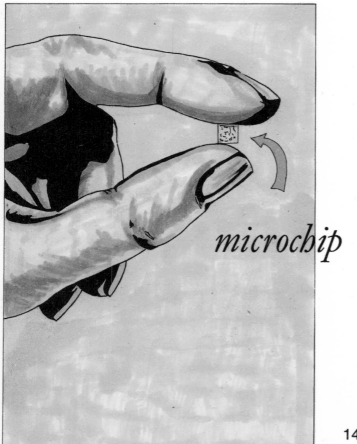

microchip

In 1948 the transistor was invented by three American physicists, William B Shockley, Walter H Brattain and John Bardeen. The use of transistors has led to the development of smaller and smaller computers.

The micro processor (microchip) was invented in 1969 by an American called E Hoff.

Mass-produced calculators first went on sale in America in 1971.

The first home computers were produced in 1975.

Communications

The first pens were probably used by the Egyptians about 3500 BC. They were made from hollow reeds and the ink was a mixture of soot and water.

Quill pens made from sharpened feathers were used from about 500 BC.

The first pencils were in use about 1565. They were made of graphite held in sticks of wood.

Fountain pens were first produced in 1884 by the American, L Waterman.

The ball-point pen was invented in 1938 by the Hungarian, Ladislao Biro.

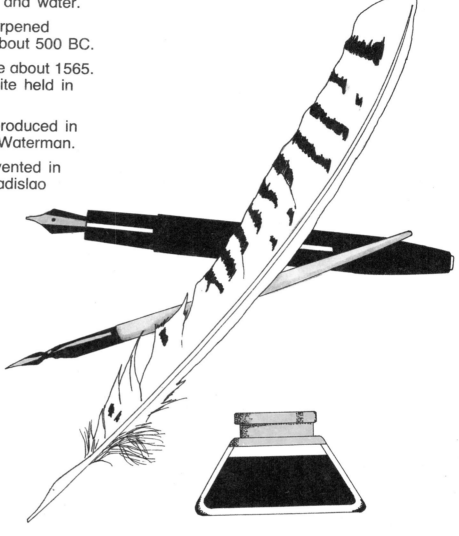

From about 800 AD the Chinese were printing pages for books using carved wooden blocks. By about 1500 they had developed movable metal type.

In 1454 the German inventor Johannes Gutenberg designed the first printing press using movable type.

Photocopiers were first developed in the USA in 1938, from a design by C Lester Carlson.

145

The first modern typewriter was built by the American inventor Christopher L Scholes. The first word-processor was produced in 1964 by IBM (USA).

The Scottish-born American scientist Alexander Graham Bell (1847–1942) invented the telephone in 1876.

The first telephone exchange was opened in 1878 in Connecticut (USA).

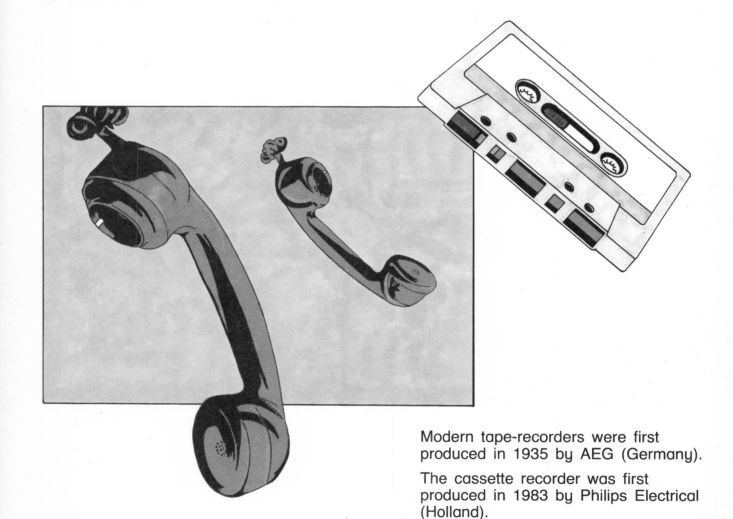

Modern tape-recorders were first produced in 1935 by AEG (Germany).

The cassette recorder was first produced in 1983 by Philips Electrical (Holland).

Compact discs were introduced in 1982 by Sony (Japan) and Philips.

The 'Penny Black', the world's first pre-paid postage stamp, was issued by the Post Office in Great Britain in 1840.

People who study and collect stamps are called philatelists.

Clothing

About 2500 BC people wore leather sandals (shoes). Clothes were held together by toggles (string loops fastened over buttons).

In 1823 when Charles Macintosh (UK) invented a new waterproof cloth he was anxious to protect the secret of its production. Therefore he chose Highland workers to work in his Glasgow factory as they only spoke Gaelic. The cloth was made into the first raincoats, known as 'macintoshes'.

The safety-pin was invented by an American named W Hunt in 1849.

The first 'jeans' were produced in America by J Davis and Levi Strauss.

The zip fastener was invented in 1891 by an American named Whitcomb Judson.

The first sewing machine was invented in 1830 by a Frenchman named Thimonnier.

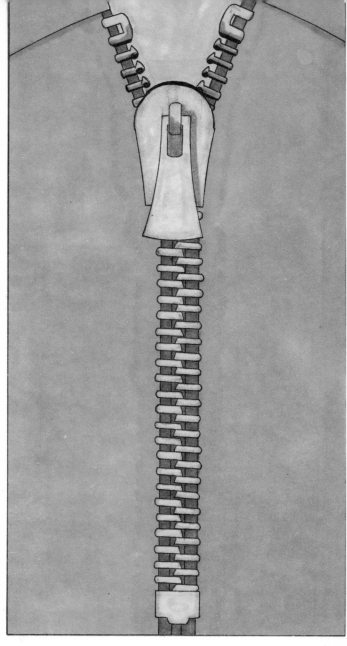

About Food

Bread was first made about 10,000 years ago in Northern Iraq. An alcoholic drink, something like beer, was being brewed about 8,000 years ago in the Middle East.

In England in the early 1700s Jethro Tull invented the first seed drill which planted seed more efficiently and improved crop yields.

The first bottled foods were produced in France about 1804.

The first canned foods went on sale in the UK in the 1820s but the can-opener was not invented until 1855. That is believed to have been designed by an Englishman called Yates.

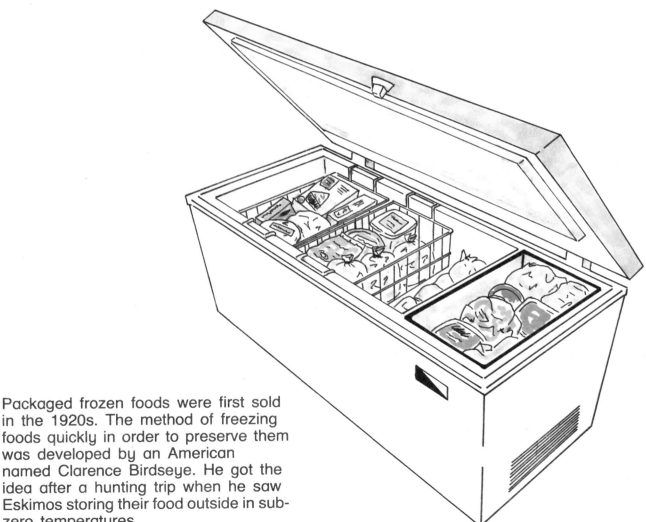

Packaged frozen foods were first sold in the 1920s. The method of freezing foods quickly in order to preserve them was developed by an American named Clarence Birdseye. He got the idea after a hunting trip when he saw Eskimos storing their food outside in sub-zero temperatures.

Household Appliances

The first domestic refrigerator was made in Germany in 1879 by K Von Linde.

The first electric vacuum cleaner was designed by A Booth (UK) in 1901.

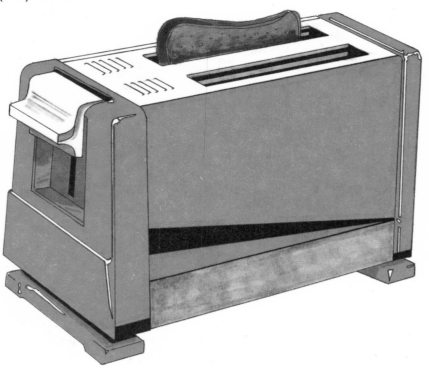

The first electric toaster was made in 1909 by the General Electric Company in America.

The first electric kettle was designed in 1923 by A Large of Great Britain.

The microwave oven was invented in the late 1940s.

Medical Discoveries and Inventions

The Greek doctor Hippocrates (460–377 BC) is known as the 'Father of Medicine'. He insisted upon scientific observation and detailed record-keeping of each illness he came across. His findings are still read and referred to by today's medical profession.

About 1267 the English monk and scholar, Roger Bacon, described a hand-held magnifying glass. By about 1280 the first spectacles were in use in Italy. They had one lens and were held in the hand. Spectacles with two lenses, which rested on the nose, came into use in the 1500s.

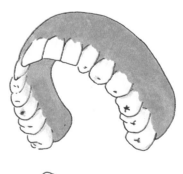

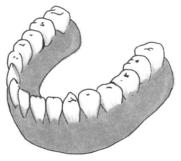

The first contact lenses were produced in Switzerland in 1887. They were made of glass. Plastic contact lenses were first produced in the USA in the late 1930s.

About 700 BC false teeth made from bone or ivory were being worn by the Ancient Etruscans of Northern Italy.

By the late 1700s comfortable porcelain dentures were being produced in France.

Galileo Galilei (1564–1642) designed a type of thermometer in 1592. It was used to measure the temperature of air. By 1654 the first sealed thermometer had been produced in Italy. It was now possible to measure the blood heat of human beings.

The Farenheit temperature scale (°F) was devised in 1718 by Daniel Farenheit (Germany). The Celsius (Centigrade) temperature scale (°C) was devised in 1742 by Anders Celsius (Sweden).

The first stethoscope was designed in 1816 by a Frenchman called René Laënnec.

Antoni van Leeuwenhoek (Holland) made one of the first successful microscopes in 1683. It had a powerful and accurate lens to view tiny objects.

X-rays were discovered in 1895 by the German physicist Wilhelm Konrad Röntgen.

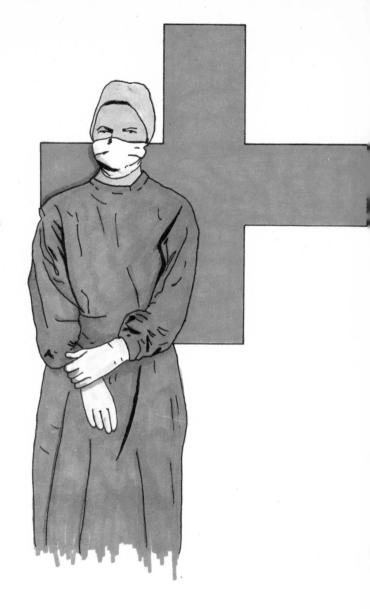

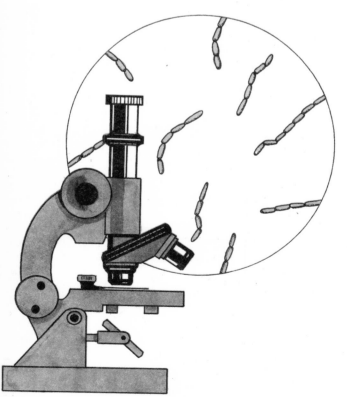

MICROSCOPE

In 1846 the first operation using ether as an anaesthetic was performed at Massachusetts General Hospital (USA). A dentist named William Morton gave the anaesthetic but the idea came from experiments carried out in 1800 by the English scientist Sir Humphrey Davy. He discovered that by using anaesthetics it was possible to make a person safely unconscious for a short period of time.

Sir Joseph Lister (1827–1912) was an English surgeon who pioneered the use of carbolic antiseptic sprays to kill germs and so prevent the spread of infection in hospitals. He introduced rules of hygiene and cleanliness.

In 1796 the English physician Edward Jenner gave the first vaccination. He successfully immunized a boy against smallpox.

The American doctor Jonas Salk developed the first poliomyelitis (polio) vaccine in 1954.

The hypodermic syringe was invented by a Frenchman named Pravaz in 1853.

The first successful kidney transplant was performed in the USA in 1950.

In South Africa in 1967 Christiaan Barnard performed the first heart transplant operation.

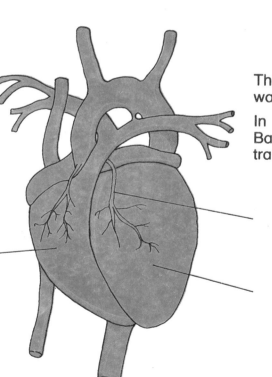

CORONARY ARTERY

RIGHT VENTRICLE

LEFT VENTRICLE

THE HUMAN HEART

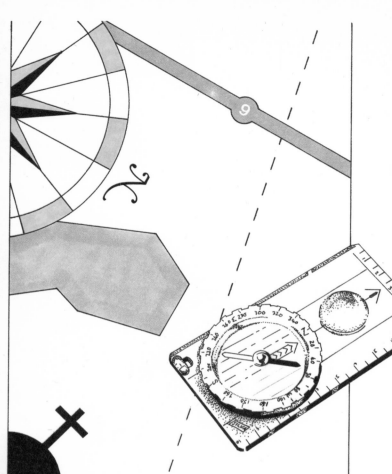

The Compass

About 500 BC the Greeks discovered how to make simple compasses using magnetic iron ore.

The magnetic compass was invented in China about 900 years ago. A magnetic needle was floated in a bowl of water. Any magnetic needle allowed to turn freely will always come to rest pointing in a North–South direction.

By 1180 the compass was in use in Europe.

SONAR – Sound Navigation and Ranging

In 1917 the French physicist Paul Langevin developed a system of echo location and called it sonar. It is used to detect underwater objects.

RADAR – Radio Detection and Ranging

The first radar set was built in Great Britain in 1931. By 1935 radar could be used to follow the path of aircraft.

LASER – Light Amplification by Stimulated Emission of Radiation

The first laser was built in 1960 by an American named Theodore H Maiman. Laser beams can be used in many different kinds of work such as delicate surgery or for cutting metals. Lasers have been used to measure vast distances and to guide bombs.

ROBERT WATSON-WATT
INVENTOR OF RADAR

Astrolabe

The first astrolabe was probably invented by the Greek astronomer Hipparchus about 150 BC. It was an instrument used to calculate the height of the sun, moon and stars above the horizon and the distances between them. Astrolabes were the main instrument used by astronomers until the telescope was invented.

ASTROLABE

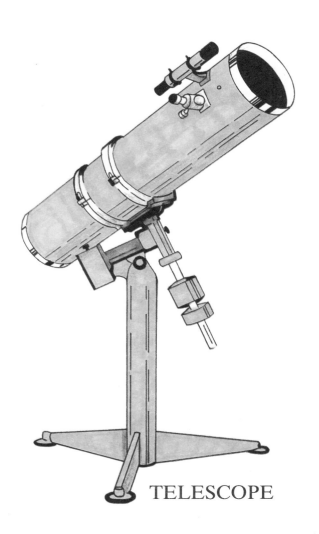

TELESCOPE

Telescopes

The first telescope was designed in 1608 by a Dutchman named Lippershey. It used lenses and was called a refracting telescope. Isaac Newton invented the reflecting telescope in 1668. It used mirrors, not lenses, and clearer images were formed. Modern telescopes are reflecting telescopes.

The largest reflecting telescope in the world was built in the Caucasus Mountains in the USSR in 1969. Its largest mirror is 6m (236 in) across.

Radio Telescopes

The first radio telescope with a dish reflector was built in 1937 by an American engineer called Grote Reber. Radio telescopes collect radio waves and focus them on the telescope's receiver.

The largest radio telescope in the world was built in 1953. It is at Arecibo (Puerto Rico). The dish is 305m (1000 ft) wide. It is a fixed telescope.

The Jodrell Bank radio telescope in England was built in 1957. It is a movable telescope and can cover greater areas of sky.

NINTH MONTH – OCTOBER
THE DOG

About Time

Thousands of years ago people used the position of the moon and the sun in the skies to work out the seasons and the best time to plant and harvest their crops.

By about 2,800 BC the Egyptians had invented a calendar to keep track of time.

Today, most people in the western world use a calendar which starts from the birth of Jesus Christ. There are others such as the Jewish and Chinese calendars which start from a different date.

The First Clocks

About 4000 years ago the Egyptians invented shadow clocks. The sundial came into use about 700 BC.

The Romans used sand clocks in the first century AD.

Candle clocks were first used in the 800s.

The first pendulum clock was made in Holland about 1650.

The first wrist watches were made in Switzerland in 1790.

Quartz wrist watches were first produced in Japan around 1967.

A SUNDIAL

What Next?

1. Scientists think that icebergs could be used to supply fresh water in desert areas. Giant tugs could be built to tow icebergs, some as much as 11.26km (7 miles) long and 2.4km ($1\frac{1}{2}$ miles) wide, from the Arctic regions. A journey to the Atacama desert in Chile could take six months but only about half of the iceberg would have melted on the way.

2. Work on the development of space planes has already begun. They will be capable of flying more than ten times faster than the speed of sound. The journey from London (England) to Tokyo (Japan) would take less than an hour.

3. People may be living on the moon in the 21st century or in space cities which will circle the Earth.